IT TAKES A
CAT BURGLAR

A THIEF IN LOVE ROMANCE

Cailin Briste

HotSaucePublishing.com

IT TAKES A CAT BURGLAR

ISBN-13 9780998912523

Editor: Lea Schafer

Cover Artist: Cailin Briste

Published in the United States of America

Hot Sauce Publishing

PO Box 13508

Offutt AFB, NE 68113-0508

www.hotsaucepublishing.com

This e-book is a work of fiction. While reference might be made to actual historical events or existing locations, the names, characters, places and incidents are either the product of the author's imagination or are used fictitiously, and any resemblance to actual persons, living or dead, business establishments, events, or locales is entirely coincidental.

Warning

This e-book contains sexually explicit scenes and adult language and may be considered offensive to some readers. Hot Sauce Publishing's e-books are for sale to adults ONLY, as defined by the laws of the country in which you made your purchase. Please store your files wisely, where they cannot be accessed by under-aged readers.

DEDICATION

For my mother, the standard for perseverance.

ACKNOWLEDGMENTS

To all the people who offer encouragement and advice through email, Facebook groups, and other online venues, I couldn't have produced this novella without you. Thank you.

To my editor, Lea Shafer, once again you've made my story better and my writing better. I was truly blessed the day I discovered your website and, with a combination of fear and hope, sent you my first manuscript. The Lord bless and keep you.

To Dr. K, the love my life, you make me feel treasured each and every day. Life with you has been a grand adventure.

CHAPTER ONE

DARCELLE'S REFLECTION STARED back at her from the solid mirror that covered the side of the Jepsen Building where she hung, suspended twelve hundred feet above the city sidewalk. Anger and determination filled the charcoal-gray eyes of her mirror image. Even as an infant, the darkness integral to her nature must have peered out of round, solemn baby eyes that weren't the expected dark brown of her mother and father or the amber of her twin sister. No, she'd been born with eyes best described as a grayish mist. With each passing year, they'd grown darker. Someday they might rival the night sky that tonight was a wash of black pushed back by the ineffectual streetlights below and the pale serenity of a waning moon. The skull cap she wore covered the braids she'd used to tame her masses of kinky cinnamon curls.

No breeze stirred the night air, for which she was thankful. The micro-cable anchored to the sidewalk didn't allow for much sway as the winch above pulled her higher. The noise of traffic wafted up like a soundtrack to another reality.

She swung a leg over the ledge surrounding the roof of the building. Sunrise was less than an hour away, but for now, the wealthy residents of the Jepsen slept below her, convinced that the security they spent thousands of credits on created an impenetrable barrier around them. She smirked, satisfied she was about to prove them wrong. The latest antiskimmer technology may prevent aircars from landing, but it didn't keep out birds or, as in her case, people who avoided the domed security field by slipping under it at the edge of the building's roof.

Security plans always had holes. Her day job at the *Art et Antiquités Institut de la Sécurité* was to close those she discovered in her client's protection profiles, or at least render them too small to be exploited. Your average cat burglar couldn't accomplish what she was attempting. The mirrored facade of the building resisted any attachments, so any of the standard slick surface anchors were worthless, as were the nonslip soles of her shoes. It was worse than trying to climb on ice.

Over the last year Darcelle had honed her skills to surpass those of the typical thief. The instructions she received before each job had included training exercises and detailed steps for committing each robbery. It was as though she was being mentored by a master thief, a man she'd never seen much less met or spoken with. Notes were his sole means of communication, written in a flowing script that was both masculine and artistic.

This was the most difficult assignment she'd received. She couldn't land on the top of the building, she couldn't climb the side, and attempting to penetrate through an entrance was equally impossible. Not a problem.

The surface of the roof was covered in fine-grain sand. She dropped from the ledge, squatting to avoid skidding and falling on her ass. The bands of her harness burned as though they were embedded in her skin. She snapped the releases and pulled the harness off, rubbing between her legs and over her lower butt cheeks. The painful part of this operation was over. She let the harness fall next to the winch. When the break-in was discovered, they'd find the hoist chem-sealed to the ledge of the Jepsen's roof. Let the security guards figure that out. It hadn't taken her long the previous night to use a gravity drone to slip it under the security field and drop it onto the ledge. The breakable containers filled with chems on the winch's underside had smashed, allowing the contents to mix and bond the winch to the stone, and the hoist had been ready to use.

She turned, squinting across the roof at an aircar circling in the distance. *Time to get indoors.* The heat tap was to her left and, next to it, the entrance to the main utility conduit. The cap had a standard entry lock, but the keypad was on the inside. Tough luck if the cover shut and you got stuck up here, unless you had the gadget she had tucked in her pocket. In less than thirty seconds it ran through a gazillion keystroke variations, and the cap popped open. She swung inside, bracing her feet on a rung of the synthsteel ladder that scaled the conduit from top to bottom. The cover thunked when she pulled it closed. Her destination wasn't far.

She stopped her descent and clamped one hand tightly on the textured metal of the ladder. With the other hand she pulled the hood of her used hazard suit over her face and sealed it. Ugh! Nothing smelled like the stale odor of air inhaled through secondhand hazard suit filters, but it was better than breathing in the poisonous air she'd be entering.

No one was supposed to be home in the penthouse. Sand nits had invaded the CEO of Trans Vargas Shipping's lofty domain. Once established, the only way to get rid of the bugs was fumigation. Who would have thought the anonymous floral bouquet sent to the man's wife would be infested with nasty critters? Threat assessment of deliveries didn't include scanning for the hundreds of tiny little eggs waiting to hatch and release a horde of pernicious pests. After all, the flowers were organic, and they weren't meant to be eaten. Thoughts of sand nits made her back itch, right in the center along her bra strap where she'd once been bitten by the nasty buggers.

Gah! Not real!

She wrenched her mind back and climbed through the hatch into the dark utility room. "Lights." Her voice was muffled by her hood and the sound-dampening walls. Across the narrow room crowded with the mech required to create modern luxury, a door led out to the main apartment. She'd taken a set of the original Jepsen Building plans from the *Bureau de la Conformité de la Construction*. Over the last week she'd memorized the route she would follow and alternates. She'd learned the hard way to do just-in-case planning when her third venture outside the law had taken a turn for the worse.

The utility room was in the staff area of the suite off a short hall that led to a swinging door. It was the dividing line between the haves from the have-nots. She hadn't grown up on the haves' side of such doors, but once her sister made tubs of money, she'd learned her way around the other side. She loped to the door, cracked it open, and scanned the serving foyer. The safe she planned to crack was in the study. That room had two entrances, one from the main hall that connected the bedrooms and another that opened from inside the master bedroom. She'd chosen the second route even though it was longer. Retrieving the item in the safe was only part of the reason for breaking and entering this luxurious home. Her primary purpose was to find what the mastermind behind her crimes had promised to leave her.

His instructions detailed the location and description of a valuable piece of art or an antiquity she was to reacquire and return to the person or institution designated. All of them had been stolen. This was her twenty-ninth burglary. Once the artifact was restored to its legitimate owner, a clue to the mystery that dominated her existence was delivered. Who was sending the notes? Why had he chosen her? She never discovered how the messages and the clues ended up where she could find them. Sometimes they were in the desk drawer in her office at work. One she found stuck to the mirror in her bathroom. Whoever was sending them was an expert cat burglar. He'd made it evident he had free run of her personal and business space. She'd nicknamed him Matou, tomcat, for obvious reasons.

Tonight's initial task, scaling the Jepsen Building, was the toughest task she'd so far encountered. Opening the safe would be easy. She could crack any safe made. You might as well gift wrap your valuables if you relied on a safe to keep burglars from walking off with them. This time her instructions had included no how-tos, just where and when. And sniggering information about sand nits. Figuring out how to get into the penthouse suite was up to her. He'd increased the difficulty.

He'd also told her this was her final exam. Whatever that meant. And after she recovered the artifact, she would find a reward waiting where the master laid his head at night. Okay. Look on the pillows of the bed in the master bedroom.

Now the end was in sight, through the entrance to the penthouse master bedroom that stood before her.

She swung the door open soundlessly. The bed was against the far wall. It had been stripped of bedding and covered with a large gray sheet. A single pillow lay at the head, a bright yellow piece of paper visible on it. The ancient Viking knife in the safe was supposed to be her priority, but she'd check the pillow first. Matou wouldn't know she'd switched things up.

She strode to the bed, her pulse pounding in her ears.

Four words. That's all that was written on the paper in the same ornate handwriting used on every preceding communication.

Congratulations. I'm behind you.

She froze.

How could she have missed it? The same dark, prickling tension that had inched along her spine every time she'd sensed Matou observing her in the past was now knitting her muscles and bones together, turning her to stone. It was him. He'd never let her see or hear him, but her body reacted when he was near, as though when he gazed at her, a furnace ignited inside her. It was damn spooky.

She jumped when his fingers closed on her shoulder.

"Don't turn."

Like a low, throbbing bass note, his voice resonated through her to the ends of her fingers. *Hell.* She couldn't move, much less turn. He trailed his hand along her collarbone. Despite the thick layer of duracloth between her and his fingertips, Darcelle was certain warmth penetrated the fabric.

His sudden yank startled her. Shock pulsed through her. He was undoing the seal on the hood of her skin suit.

"No!" She batted at him, twisting to escape his grasp. He clamped her in a bruising hold, immobilizing her.

"I said don't turn. Stop struggling."

Rapid inhalations of the sour combination of aged body odor and fear inside her skin suit made her nasal passages burn. She continued to writhe, fighting to free herself. *He's going to kill me!*

"Fuck it. Stop. The air is pure. Look."

Several moments passed before she registered the sun-darkened arm and hand waving in front of her. Long elegant fingers twiddled. Her breathing hitched. No gloves. He wasn't wearing a skin suit. She stilled, allowing him to remove her hood.

"Do exactly as I say, and all will be well."

With gentler hands he turned her toward him. She gasped. He was gorgeous. Only a master sculptor could have formed a face of such perfect symmetry. The masculinity of his high cheekbones, angled jaw, and straight brows was softened by his exquisite lips. Heat flushed through her body.

From beneath black locks slanting over his forehead, pale green eyes stared at her. Was he waiting for a response?

"Ummm."

A smile flashed across his lips. "Are you ready to trust me?"

Darcelle pursed her lips. "I'll try."

He grunted. "Good enough. We are alike, minou, my kitten. Our trust must be earned."

In the silence that fell, Darcelle waited, her legs growing restless. An instant before she burst into anxious questions, he spoke.

"This skin suit is repulsive. Clothes have been laid out for you in the master bathroom. I assume you know where that is located?"

She nodded her head, trying to keep her respiration steady even though her chest was tight. This calm, gorgeous man, her cat burglar, her Matou, had her flustered and, beyond all belief, compliant.

"Change and meet me in the study."

"Yes, Mat—"

Her confusion must have shone on her face, because he filled in the missing designation. "Sir. Call me sir." He quirked an eyebrow at her.

Darcelle dropped her gaze to the floor. "Yes, sir."

"Go on."

She heard a smile in his voice. When she looked up, his lips were twitched in a half grin. She returned his expression before skittering off toward the bathroom. *Gods, he's so damn hot!*

CHAPTER TWO

DARCELLE STEELED HERSELF before entering the study. She'd been shocked to discover her own clothes laid out for her. This stranger had insinuated himself deep into her life, and she was determined to find out why.

He was seated at a large desk, hands behind his head, long legs stretched before him, and feet propped on the desktop. *Arrogant man.* Before her strides brought her to stand across from him, he pointed at a chair positioned at an angle to the desk. It was straight in line with his gaze, so he could study her at his ease.

"Sit there." He returned his hands to the back of his head.

Darcelle ignored the command, stopping at the edge of the desk. "Who are you?"

A glimmer of heat flashed. "If you want your questions answered, you will sit. Do not defy me. There will be consequences."

Unmoved by the threat, she pressed her lips in a tight line and narrowed her eyes. If it was a battle of wills he wanted, she'd be happy to oblige.

He stared pointedly at her. "Do you want answers?"

She balled her hands into fists. He had her. Without looking at him, she sat.

"Good girl."

She shot her gaze up to him. *Gods. I'd like to wipe that smirk from your face. Or kiss it away.* What the hell was wrong with her? She should look out for herself not sink deeper under his thrall.

He abruptly dropped his feet to the floor and sat forward, his gaze aimed so sharply at her that she jerked back.

"There's a price for my services. It's time for you to pay."

Heat bloomed through Darcelle. What did he mean? Hadn't she been serving him this whole time?

He rose and moved to stand behind her, placing his dexterous fingers on her shoulders and gently massaging her taut muscles. Head tipped to the side, she succumbed to his ministrations even though she ought to resist. Over the last year she'd dreamed of him seducing her, and now the man of her most erotic fantasies was rubbing his hands over her. A tremor coursed through her body.

He nuzzled soft lips against her check and whispered, "That's better."

Resistance had drained away. He clasped her hand and led her to a sofa. "Sit with me."

Darcelle sat at one end of the sofa. A faint gasp fell from her lips when he positioned himself next to her, his thigh touching hers. She dropped her gaze to her russet, reddish-brown fingers engulfed in his warm beige hand. When he spoke, she looked once again into his eyes, her heart thudding.

"I'm an artist of sorts. A dilettante. I abhor that the wealthy keep so many of the universe's masterpieces to themselves. I cannot change that, but I can recover works that have been stolen from venues open to the public."

With one finger he brushed a trail from her temple to her jaw. "I rescue beautiful things." A smile played along his lips, and he withdrew his hand.

"I need a partner. You."

Darcelle's mouth fell open. "What?"

He smirked. "I'd been looking for some time when I discovered you."

One question moved through Darcelle's mind like sludge. *Discovered me?* She was pulled back to the conversation when Matou squeezed her hand.

"You surpassed my expectations."

"Did I?"

His gaze softened. "Yes. You've passed your initial training, but more will be required before we can work together. Once you've completed the next phase, you may decide whether to join me. If you choose to, you can leave now, and I will never contact you again."

"What does the next phase involve?"

"You'll be learning the rules I require of anyone who works with me. A series of tests will help me decide where to focus your training. Simulations will play an important part in preparing you to be *under* me. It shouldn't take more than a month."

Under him. Gods, she wanted to be under him. Had he meant what that word implied? Her nipples tingled. *Stop it! This is your life. It's more than getting laid.*

Considerations raced through her mind. One more month and she could be done with this whole thing. Or not. What was another thirty days of cat burglary? Her clandestine adventures had offered the most fun she'd ever had. She didn't want to quit. But could she handle going solo? She slid her gaze over Matou. He wasn't just a handsome face. He was built like a sleek black panther, lean, muscular, and thrumming with lethal energy. What would it hurt to discover what this mortally alluring man had in store for her?

"I agree."

Matou tipped his chin up and looked down at her. "Take time to think about it."

"I've thought. I agree. But, you must allow me to continue to work. I can't lose my job."

He dropped his chin, his gaze blazing with heated satisfaction, and grinned wickedly at her. "I can arrange a leave of absence from the *Institut* for you. I will pay your usual salary while you are with me."

"Okay." The butterflies attacking her stomach were 20 percent apprehension, 75 percent anticipation, and a 5 percent dollop of good old-fashioned lust.

He picked up a packet from a side table and handed it to her. "Here is the knife you came for. You were to retrieve it first. In future, if you do not adhere to my instructions, you will be punished. Use your escape route to leave. I'll dispose of your skin suit. You won't need that shabby relic again."

Her eyes widened. "This really was a burglary?"

"I wouldn't waste your time or mine." He rose, pulling her hand up with him and waiting for her to stand.

She was nearly his equal in height. He caught her with his pale green gaze, mesmerizing her. Could he see inside her? Read her mind? She was laid bare before him. Who she was and what she believed, everything was open for him to examine and to judge. Gods, she wanted to be worthy of him.

He leaned in and brushed his mouth across hers. Those artfully sculpted lips were touching her. She accepted the caress, her body both rigid and boneless at the same time.

He pulled away, and the loss was painful. She needed more.

"We need to leave, minou. You'll be hearing from me." When she didn't move, he stepped beside her, placed his palm firmly on her bottom, and scooted her forward. "*À la prochaine.*"

Yes. She couldn't wait until next time. She turned at the study door and looked back over her shoulder, but he was gone. Damn, he was quiet. Giddiness flooded her. She would train with a master cat burglar, be his partner. And that kiss... Her mind filled with various activities that could follow that kiss. She wound through the apartment to the utility room, out the hatch into the main utility conduit, and up the ladder. With her harness once more in place, she latched it to the hoist's micro-cable and slipped over the edge of the roof, holding the package containing the knife tightly in one hand against her body. Once again on the ground, she detached the line and sent it back. Her harness was off in a minute. She wrapped it around the package and headed home. It wasn't until then that she remembered she still didn't know Matou's name.

SEBASTIAN RETURNED TO sit behind the desk. For long minutes he didn't move except for the thumb he rubbed across his lower lip. Today had gone as planned. He'd expected Darcelle to enter the penthouse undetected, and she'd succeeded. Her solution to the problem had been technically precise, something he anticipated from her. She didn't rely on subterfuge to the extent he did, which made her an ideal partner. Her strengths complemented his.

But over the last year, the degree to which she was his counterbalance had become steadily more apparent. She was his match. Someone he had never envisaged finding. And he wanted her more than he'd desired anything else in his life. That she would accept his proposition to train with him for a month hadn't been in any real doubt. The hook had been set early. In the ensuing months he'd allowed her to believe she was still in charge of her destiny, but the time had come to reel her in. And that would be trickier.

All his plans depended on Darcelle joining him. It was too late to find someone else. Experienced cat burglars didn't advertise their services. Jeanne and Cheyenne's happiness counted on this partnership.

He launched himself from the chair, stooped, and pulled out the coverall and cap from under the desk where he'd stowed them. Time was running short. With the shoes he'd borrowed from the penthouse owner's closet removed, he slipped the coverall over his clothes and put on his work boots. The cap was added after he'd rumpled his hair.

Once the shoes and any other items that had been displaced were set to rights, he reset the interior security cameras. He assumed the role of workman, shambling though the rooms in the penthouse, scuffing his boots on the plush carpets and lustrous wood and tile floors, and plugging the ventilation intakes and registers.

At the main entry, the knob rattled. He disengaged the lock he'd placed on the door with his personal ident. He hadn't wanted the workers on the other side to get impatient, as they clearly had, and enter the penthouse before he was ready for them.

The heavyset foreman glared at him. "Why'd you lock the door?"

Sebastian responded in an unhurried manner, his voice set a pitch higher than normal. "Didn't."

"Well I couldn't get it open."

"I dunno. Wasn't me locked it. But you ain't got no right comin' inside. That's my job. I'll call my union rep you try that on me. See if

I don't."

The foreman fisted his hands. "I can check on you. That's my job. What took so long? The sun's almost up, and we have to be out of here by noon."

"Yeah, had to fix some stuff. They left out food in the kitchen. And the main intake was bigger than we was told, so I had to work at gettin' the cover to fit. Finally got it."

"Whatever. You were playing around in there. Now we have to make up for the time you lost us." He turned to scowl at the other man with him. "Get started with the door. And make sure this asshole"—he pointed at Sebastian—"doesn't waste any more time."

Sebastian bent to grab one side of the door while the other crew member removed its hinges. He smiled to himself. It had been simple to pay off a worker and assume his spot. Neither the foreman nor the other worker were aware that the owner of their company was assisting them today, especially since said owner was hidden behind several layers of corporate entities. Manipulation and subterfuge were Sebastian's preferred method when planning a burglary. This setup had allowed him to enter the penthouse alone as the union worker assigned to interior work and to destroy all evidence that he had been here once the decontamination was finished. Perfect.

When the door was fully released, Sebastian and the crew member set it to the side against the outer foyer wall. The other man squatted over the box, holding the framework they would secure around the opening, and gave Sebastian a furtive glance. "Did you take somethin'?" he whispered.

"Nah. What would I do that for? I ain't got no use for that fancy stuff."

"You could sell it."

"To who? Eh. I'd get caught for sure. My cousin spent time for breaking and entering. I promised my mom I wouldn't be like him. I'm doin' fine as I am."

The other man grunted, his expression suggesting Sebastian was a moron.

The foreman who'd been leaning against the wall and messing

with his handheld raised his head. "Get on with it, dickheads."

Smirking wouldn't be in character, so Sebastian said, "Sure thing, boss." The foreman's attitude would get annoying before the day was over. But the aggravation was worth it. Darcelle had finished the initial training regimen Sebastian had designed for her, and the Viking knife would soon be on its way to the Earth Heritage Museum. He wouldn't let this highly successful day be ruined by a jackass.

CHAPTER THREE

IT HAD BEEN TWO DAYS since Darcelle had met Matou in person. She'd tried to follow her normal routine but accomplished little. Why the hell did he have to give her so much time to reconsider? One minute she was telling herself she was crazy to accept his offer. The next minute fantasies about what his training might entail stoked her excitement. But when doubt assailed her, that kiss tipped her back onto the go-for-it side of the what-should-she-do equation.

Her comm signaled. It was her mother. Not a good time to listen to another harangue about lack of family loyalty. But if she didn't answer now, the calls would increase in frequency until she did.

"Hello, Mother."

"I can't believe I got through to you. You never take my comms and never return my messages."

"Sorry." Darcelle held back a sigh.

"You should be. What if it was an emergency? Your sister could be in an accident, in hospital, and you'd never know. Too busy for either of us."

"Why did you call, Mother?"

"Your sister has gotten the lead role in *La Passionelle*. Think of it. The *Théâtre de l'Odéon*. You'll have to quit your job and go with her. You're the only one that can make sure that every detail of her life is in proper order. Her focus on this part cannot be disturbed in any way. I've already booked tickets and packed an appropriate wardrobe for you. You'll leave—"

"Mother…"

"In two—"

"Mother, I'm not going."

"Don't be ridiculous. Of course you're going. Your sister needs you."

"No, she doesn't. She has plenty of staff to fetch and carry for her. I have my own life now. I've told you I won't be Cassie's personal assistant any longer. Please stop asking me to do things you know I won't do."

"You wretched girl. You have no gratitude for everything that Cassie and I have done for you. I don't know how a daughter of mine could be so self-involved, so ready to repudiate the family that loves her. You'll change your tune when you need us. When you lose that trivial little job of yours."

"Mother, I have to go. I'm quite busy."

"Busy! Too busy for your own mother, your own sister. Fine."

Darcelle's EBC signaled her mother had ended the comm. *Fine.* She rubbed her forehead. Her mother would never change. Never understand that Darcelle had at last found something she was good at. That it involved criminal activity was fitting. She, as her mother had proclaimed often, was the dark one in a family where white-collar pseudo-crime, perpetrated to better your position in the world, was fine. Not the blue-collar breaking and entering Darcelle had discovered an ability for. You could steal an opportunity from another budding starlet through deceptive means, but never take her diamond tiara.

Not that she'd awakened one morning determined to become a cat burglar. No, she'd been seduced into it. Matou and his notes. At first she'd refused to take his written messages with their tasks and promises seriously. But the notes had continued to appear along with notices from the newsies, showing that whether she'd accepted a job or not, it was still accomplished. He taunted her that hiding in her little office at the *Institut* did nothing to restore stolen treasures to the public. Why should she care? It wasn't her responsibility to investigate such crimes. She assured the security of the *Institut's* clients. But she did care. How could she not be frustrated when other companies' protection measures were breeched and valuable artwork or artifacts were stolen? It made her mad. But not angry enough to commit crimes to steal the items back.

Then Matou's fifth note appeared on her bedside table. It required Darcelle to crash a party and take a vid of a man standing before a stolen painting. Her instructions included the type of hidden vid cam to use and the pass code to the party. It looked easy. And legal. What could it hurt? Once she'd commed the vid to the proper authorities, another note arrived.

Well done, minou. Did you tingle with exhilaration or fear? Exhilaration, I think. You were born to be bold, to hunt like the striking feline woman you are. Your next mission will be even more daring. Soon, mon petit.

The note assumed she'd enjoyed deception. He was right. Goose bumps had dotted her skin. It had been a thrill to record the covert vid that exposed the person who had purchased a stolen Picasso. Darcelle was hooked.

She still didn't know his identity and why he'd chosen her to be part of this exhilarating game in which she was seriously entangled. The clues he'd left were filled with information that didn't fit together. She wanted those answers. A search of local newsie channels and datalinks hadn't turned up a thing. Why did he choose her and not some other more likely candidate to commit these crimes, to become a second Robin Hood, returning priceless treasures to the people? And the scariest question of all: now that she had progressed well past petty crime to felonies, would he be there to help if she were arrested?

If this was some fiendish game he was playing with her, she wasn't his little cat, but the fly to his spider. By the time she'd finished her third mission, she'd been thoroughly trapped. Laws had been broken. She'd nearly been caught. Even now she could end the game. He wouldn't turn her in. At least, it didn't seem likely. He'd be disappointed but not vindictive. That was moot. Her fate was sealed. She'd become addicted to the inebriating thrill of committing these sensational crimes and would continue as long as

Matou wanted to play. The call from her mother added incentive to take the next step.

She'd had plenty of time to decide what to take when he sent for her. Her travel bag was stuffed with clothes, toiletries, and anything else she could imagine she might need. That was the problem. She didn't know what that included, so she'd crammed a little of everything in: exercise, work, and casual clothes; shampoo and body lotion; burglary tools; and after much deliberation, a slinky black nightie.

Her comm pinged a message. It was Matou.

"I'm waiting for you below. Dark blue sedan. Bring nothing with you."

A void opened in the pit of her stomach. This was it. He was here. She either went to him and got in the car, or she commed him back and said she'd changed her mind. Should she? No. She shouldn't. She should go. Yes. Her suitcase. Where was it? By the door. She lifted it by the handle. No. Not supposed to take it. She slung her handbag over her shoulder. No way was she leaving it behind. Gods, just go!

With her door locked behind her, she scurried to the lift. She had to get in that car before her palpitating heart went into cardiac arrest. On the ground floor the lift opened, and she rushed past the building's security guard, barely acknowledging his greeting. A dark blue sedan waited at the curb. The driver stepped out of the vehicle and opened the passenger door for her. Inside, the lower half of a fit male body was visible, Matou. When she ducked her head to climb in, she had a full view of him. Her gaze fixated on his lips, and memories of his kiss took center stage in her thoughts. Her lungs froze. Warmth flooded through her. She'd made the right choice. Nothing would keep her from this man's side.

In a voice laced with dry humor, he said, "Are you going to get in?"

Darcelle gave her head a slight shake, trying to focus. "Yes, sir." He was better looking than any man was entitled to be. Every one of the hairs on his gleaming black head was perfectly in place except for a small tuft over his left eyebrow that refused to stay put. But that only added to the perception that he was flawless.

When she was seated, the car pulled away and Matou handed her an eye mask. "Put this on."

"You don't want me to know where we're going?"

"No."

She pursed her lips.

"Put it on, or we turn around," he said.

After a brief glance at Matou, she slipped the mask on, hoping to keep the chill skating through her veins from causing her fingers to tremble. As though he appreciated her struggle to remain calm, Matou placed his hand over hers.

"For the next month, you will live in my home. Your training will be around the clock and will involve all aspects of your life. You will eat what I tell you to eat. You will sleep when and where I tell you to sleep. Any tasks I set for you will be completed swiftly and thoroughly. I expect you to give me everything you have to give. Your physical, emotional, and mental stamina will be tested past your endurance. Together we will discover your limits, and where necessary, I will stretch you beyond them. Do you understand?"

Darcelle released the breath she'd been holding. One month. Could she spend an entire month allowing someone else to dictate how she spent every moment of her life? Freedom from expectations and demands had been the reason she had moved into her own apartment. It was her escape from a mother who believed she had the right to shape Darcelle's life. As long as she'd smothered her individuality, helping her sister pursue her acting career, Darcelle's basic needs had been met. But free food, clothes, and shelter hadn't been enough. She'd found employment, established her own circle of friends, and reveled in the ability to let her own likes and dislikes shape her personal decisions. It had been liberating, and now she was on the brink of granting Matou similar control over her.

She lifted her head to face the direction where Matou sat. It was impossible to determine his thoughts from the tone of his voice, and as for reading his expression, her vision was obscured by the fabric of the mask. "And when my training is finished, I will become your partner? Robin to your Batman?"

His hand brushed the curls that framed her face. His touch sent a pulse of desire through her. She wanted him to stroke her, to tell her she was everything he hoped she'd be. It was that need that ultimately decided her each time she questioned her decision to join him. And it was her choice. Allowing him this month to train her wasn't being forced upon her. She could reject the offer. But that would mean rejecting him, and he was the most compelling man she had ever met.

In a gravel-roughened voice, he said, "We will be the greatest cat burglar duo this planet, or possibly even this sector of the Federation, has ever seen. The term 'partner' only hints at what you will become."

Something shifted in her chest. "I want that."

He pulled a strand of her hair, stretching it to its full length, and brushed his fingers along her jawline, making her shudder.

"You are the one who will determine where your future lies. Obey me immediately and to the last detail, and you will gain everything you desire."

"Yes, sir. I understand." When she was his partner, would he finally reveal his name, who he was, and how he found her? She was one step closer to discovering the answers to those questions. If she trusted him, would he trust her? She'd already taken a leap of faith in him, but she could always leave, quit the training if things didn't work to her liking.

"We've arrived. You may remove the mask."

She did, but rather than look out the car window, she focused on him. Let him see she could control her curiosity.

His lips twitched and eyes sparkled with amusement. "Very good. You may look wherever you please."

After the driver opened the car door, Matou walked to Darcelle's side and helped her out. His hand, warm and strong, clasped hers, steadying her. She wasn't afraid. Matou didn't inspire fear in her. Her restless excitement resulted from the desire to reach her future—now. She wanted to see, feel, know everything that awaited her, and time spent on social niceties was a painful hindrance to speeding forward. But his touch brought her back in sync with his plans and timetable.

From the parking garage he escorted her into the building and to the lift. "I live in the penthouse." She acknowledged the information with a bob of her head. The lift rose after he keyed in his code. The doors slid aside to show an exotically decorated foyer. Replicas of ancient Egyptian artifacts, including a mummy case, were artfully arranged along walls embellished with Egyptian tomb paintings. Smooth columns with lotus capitals supported the stone lintels of three doorways. The two wider doors to the left and right led into reception rooms, while the one straight ahead opened on a long hall with dark rose-colored, embossed walls lined with mirrors and side tables. Each table held an exquisite piece of sculpture.

Darcelle soaked in the atmosphere, gawking at each amazing item that caught her eye. Matou's home was like a museum. The pieces weren't originals because he opposed keeping art from the people. So they must be replicas. Still expensive, high-quality copies.

"My mother designed the public areas where I receive guests. I gave her a free hand, which Papa never allowed. Thus the extravagance. Some rooms are quite gaudy." He gazed at her with an assessing look. "I didn't know I'd take in my own cinnamon Abyssinian cat, or I'd have had all the public rooms done in the Egyptian decor of the foyer, a fitting setting to display your loveliness to my guests. But those eyes tell me someone else is hidden inside you, minou. Cats don't have gray eyes."

Darcelle was unsure how to respond, so she walked beside him, while his gaze continued to rove over her. She was aware her eyes, large and almond shaped with a fringe of long, red-brown lashes, were her most striking feature. But she wanted him to see her for more than a physically attractive woman. Advice she should take herself. He wasn't just exceptionally good-looking. His bespoke suit, his unique scent, a blend of citrus, leather, and charcoal, and the elegant signet ring on his right hand pointed to the sophistication of the man wearing them.

He drew her to a door inconspicuously set in the corner of the long hall. It opened once he'd placed his palm over the ident plate that was discretely hidden behind a sliding panel that matched the wall covering.

Inside the setting was a complete contrast to the foyer and hall. The design was modern without devolving into the uniformity of the latest trend toward robotic sterility. The furnishings were uncluttered and comfortable, relying on grace of line to evoke an overall artistic effect.

"Follow me. Your bedroom is this way." Matou didn't wait for a response but headed toward a hall that led off from the living room, not giving her the opportunity to take in the dramatic view from the floor-to-ceiling windows. She hurried after him.

Her own bedroom. *Good.* Partners had separate bedrooms. Still a small flame of hope had burned inside her, lit by that kiss, hope that he would share a bed with her. *Get your mind off sex!* Hard to do when her stomach dropped every time he spoke to her or looked at her. *Gods, he doesn't even have to touch me.* When she stepped into the room, her gaze was at once drawn to and riveted by the huge bed that appeared to float in the air above a dark wooden base.

The sound of Matou clearing his throat brought her back from visions of being entwined in his arms while he forcefully penetrated her. *Damn it all to hell. You're not here to get laid.* What must he be thinking? Could he tell that she ached between her thighs? If he did, it didn't show. He was as composed as ever. *Arrogant man!*

"You will find clothes to fit you in the closet." He gestured to a pair of doors at the end of the room. "The bathroom is through the arch. Inside is a hamper for dirty clothes. Take your shoes off and place them in your closet. Go to the bathroom, strip, and place your clothes in the hamper. Wait for me there." His tone of voice was peremptory. Immediate compliance was fully implied.

Darcelle hesitated, off-balance from the tingle of pleasure his words and commanding tone gave her and the unexpected buzz of anxiety that followed. "Yes, Sir."

What was happening to her? Yes, Matou was sexy as hell. Yes, she wanted to sleep with him. Now would not be soon enough. But when he'd ordered her to strip, her reaction had been more than the usual excitement of getting naked with a handsome man. That place inside her that yowled in protest when someone attempted to dominate her had purred instead. Not a full-bodied rumble of pleasure. A barely perceptible bleat of enjoyment. But that was both new and wrong. Her arousal faded.

It had taken her years to throw off her mother's control. The possibility that she might allow Matou to take up the reins she'd pulled from her mother's grasp had seemed remote—until that spark of satisfaction had tugged at something buried inside her. It wasn't physical attraction. It was something else. Was this what Matou had seen hidden in her eyes? If so, she would resist it. She was to be his partner, his cat burgling partner. One month under his complete control and she would be his equal. No one would dominate her again. *Gods.* She would have to be careful. Succumbing to his sex appeal would be the first step to allowing him to subjugate her.

She moved toward the closet Matou had pointed to when he left the bedroom. The closet's automatic lights blinked on, revealing a large room. Round racks took up most of the space, holding clothing for every imaginable activity. One wall was covered with niches filled with shoes and boots. An oversize armchair was positioned next to a side table before a semicircle mirror. Two tall dressers stood on either side of it.

This room and its contents were for her. She drifted toward the closest rack and fingered a bright green silk blouse. Expensive. To proclaim her autonomy, she'd given up a free wardrobe. The apparel was nice, more than nice, luxurious. But she'd never needed pretty clothes. Not like her sister had. This at least was no temptation.

She shook herself from her reverie. Her promise had been immediate obedience for this month, and she wasn't starting out well. With a double flick of toe to heel, she removed her shoes. One cubby stood empty, so she placed the flats, her preferred footwear, in it and hurried to the bathroom.

Decadence surrounded her. A sunken white marble tub large enough for several tall adults to stretch out in occupied the far corner. The perfect tub for an up-to-her-neck protracted soak in floral-scented bubbles. The view from it was nothing less than spectacular. Vid screens made to resemble windows lined any extra wall space. They were set to replicate scenery viewed from a sunny villa nestled in the hills of a vineyard overlooking a blue sea. It was as though the sunshine warmed her skin and the ocean breeze wafted the scent of salt water and baking sand through the room.

The hamper Matou had told her about was just inside the door. She quickly slipped out of her clothes, stuffing them into the receptacle, while continuing to gawk at the room's decor.

A long vanity lined the closest wall. Feminine products stood in rows on the glass shelves on either side of the vid mirror that hung above the sink. She hadn't had a vid mirror since she'd moved away from home. It wasn't so much a mirror as a live vid of the person facing the mirror. Double tap the mirror and the vid gear behind it would zoom in, allowing a close-up view for those tricky beautification moments.

She stepped to the shelves and picked up a bottle. It was an expensive brand of shampoo perfect for her hair type. The moisturizer to keep it from drying out stood next to the shampoo. Damn. Nothing was missed. Depilatory cream, nail clippers and files, and every other thing she might need were arranged in organized fashion, including one shelf filled with makeup products in the colors and formulations she preferred.

A small gadget caught her eye. She examined the tip. Was it sonic? The small touch pad next to it must control it. Before she could switch the device on, Matou entered the room. He'd changed into casual slacks and a thin sweater. The pad slipped from her fingers onto the shelf, and she hastened to cover herself. Her gaze dropped to the floor.

His voice was gruff. "Don't hide your body. You might as well get used to the fact that you'll be nude around me. I hadn't thought you'd be so modest."

Darcelle furrowed her brow, her hands falling to her sides. "I'm not usually. I don't know..." What was wrong with her? She was behaving like an inexperienced girl, not a twenty-five-year-old woman.

With a few rapid strides Matou was in front of her, gripping her upper arms and sending a tremor of need through her.

"Look at me."

She brought her gaze up to focus on his pale green eyes. How could he look so placid when his touch made her want to squirm and, gods, even rub herself against him? Then the corners of his eyes crinkled. He was as affected by this encounter as she was. If she looked at his crotch, would it be bulging now? Impossible to tell because he had captured her with his stare, and she couldn't glance away.

When his gaze moved to her lips, she hoped he would kiss her. He did, but the kiss landed on her forehead, a purely platonic act. *Damn it all to hell. How did he control himself like that?*

"You're fine. We'll start with an examination. Stand here."

What did that mean? Visual examination? Touching? Was he planning to peer into her naval? She suppressed the giggle that had bubbled up inside her. No, she wouldn't allow a case of nerves to ruin the good impression she wanted to make on him.

He led her to stand in the center of a two-foot circle, part of the pattern of the inlaid marble tile floor. Gently clasping her fingers, he stepped out of the circle's circumference and depressed a button on the remote he'd picked up. She dropped her gaze to her toes when the floor vibrated beneath her. The circle, with her on it, rose like a platform in a stage show. It stopped with her a yard higher. Why would anyone have this kind of contraption in their bathroom? Did he like his women naked on a pedestal? Wouldn't the bedroom be a better place for it?

He released her hand, tapped her ankle, and said, "Move your feet wider apart." After she complied, he smoothed a palm down her calf. "You're in good shape, but I'm starting you on a regimen that will give you better breath control and focus on flexible strength, especially in your upper body." His fingers skimmed the backs of both of her legs. He moved in front of her and inspected her feet, tracing an old scar on the top of her left foot. "What's this from?"

"I dropped a knife on my foot while I was cooking."

"I'll bet that hurt."

"It did."

This is what he'd meant by an examination. He was inspecting her, not as his potential bedmate but to determine any physical deficiencies she had that would interfere with her becoming his partner in crime. She wanted his touch, craved it. This clinical assessment was both reassuring and maddening. Hell. If he had no problem being self-composed around her nude body, she could be just as calm, cool, and collected. Her new motto. The three *c*'s.

She jumped when he pinched the finger she was unconsciously tapping against her thigh.

"Remain still." His voice was a rough growl. *So, he can be irritated too. Good. I'm not the only one.*

"Minou, you will learn to trust that I have a good reason for everything I do. Explanations will rarely follow my commands. Impatience with me will be punished. Do you understand?" His gaze drilled into her.

She pressed her lips together and wrinkled her nose. After swallowing she said, "I understand what you want from me, but—"

"But it's hard. I'm aware that this will be difficult, perhaps the most difficult thing you must learn. It is essential. I need you to do this for me."

Darcelle dropped her gaze to her toes. "Yes, Sir." He needed her to do this, to rely on his decisions. Could she do that? His words, *do this for me*, had elicited another stronger purr from that place inside her. She wanted to trust him, but her relationship with her mother proved that even those that should love you most, should want your best interests, could use you for their own purposes. If she followed that urge to immerse herself in trusting this man, would she lose herself and become something he wanted? Reason enough to be on guard.

"This time I will explain my intentions. I have an intense, fast-paced training program outlined for you. It will stress the limits of your physical abilities. Before you start, it's paramount that I know if you have any conditions that would change my plans. This is for your safety and well-being."

Her cheeks heated. "Thank you, Sir. May I…ask a question?"

He gazed up at her. "You can always ask questions."

"Why do you have a pedestal that rises from the floor in the bathroom?"

He arched an eyebrow at her. "It's a boo-boo seat."

"A boo-boo seat?"

With a bark of laughter, he explained. "My mother has always insisted on installing boo-boo seats in every bathroom, so it was easy to tend to the cuts and scrapes my brothers and I accumulated. I kept the tradition in my own home."

The platform lowered a foot, taking her by surprise. This time she didn't have his hand to lean on, but she remained steady.

"You have good balance. But I already knew that."

He ought to. The assignments he'd sent her on had included doing things that would have been impossible if she were shaky, especially where heights were concerned.

"The more I know about you, the more you remind me of a cat, minou. High places don't scare you. We'll test your leaping ability."

That was more like it. She pressed her lips together to avoid smiling.

Matou continued his inspection, touching, asking questions, and gradually lowering the pedestal until she was once again at floor level. He palmed both of her breasts, forcing her to clench her abdominal muscles to hold back a moan. *Calm, cool, collected. Calm, cool, collected.*

"You are lovely." He released her breasts, moved behind her, and scooped up her mass of kinky curls, holding them away from her neck with one hand. His lips were now close enough that his warm breath brushed across her skin. She fisted her hands.

He whispered in her ear, "Have you ever seen an Abyssinian cat? Your coloring, the almond shape of your eyes, even your ears are feline."

Cat ears? Her twin had always teased Darcelle about the size of her ears. As though Cassie's weren't as big.

"Myth says the statues of the Ancient Egyptian cat goddess, Bastet, were made in the likeness of Abyssinian cats. Bastet was a protector."

His tongue traced the curve of her ear. "That's what you will be, a protector of the people's right to their own heritage. And you'll be mine, minou."

Oh gods. He wants me. She hadn't read him wrong before. The three c's deserted her. The erogenous zones in her body were clamoring for more. If he kept her standing here, she would surely collapse.

His fingers massaged her scalp and traced along her neck to her shoulders. "Everything about you is perfect. I won't need to change my plans for you."

He stepped away, taking his warmth with him, gripped her ass, and gave it a squeeze. "You'll find a robe on the hook behind the door. Put it on and follow me."

The robe was a silky soft floral-patterned confection she fumbled to slip on. *Think about something else, anything else but him. The robe. Real silk? Maybe.* He led her out of the bedroom and toward a set of double doors. She kept her gaze riveted on the floor to avoid the temptation of staring at his butt while he walked in front of her.

CHAPTER FOUR

WITH ONE HAND Sebastian swung a door open and with the other invited Darcelle to enter. Inside, a balcony overlooked a two-story gymnasium. He took her hand, and they walked down the steps leading to the gym floor. Exercise equipment was lined up on one side of the room. One wall simulated a variety of climbing surfaces. The closest corner to the foot of the stairs held medical equipment for testing heart, lung capacity, or strength. And the standard gym med bed in case of injury.

While Darcelle scanned the gym, he kept his gaze fixed on her. He hadn't planned to depart her room as abruptly as he had, but the only other choice, the one his body urged him to make, was to throw her on her bed and take her. Concealing her enticing curves was a necessity if he was to keep to his plans. The robe covered her, but it didn't hide her shapely lines. Even now he fought the impulse to brush a hand over her backside.

At the foot of the stairs he led her toward the med station.

"Climb onto the med bed. I'm going to do a complete physical on you."

Without a word Darcelle boosted herself up and lay on the padded bed. When she scooted into position, her robe inched higher. He bit back the groan that rose inside him. Gods, he should have requested a long, frumpy chenille robe. Instead silk fabric slid over smooth skin... His fingers tingled, but rather than touching her, he averted his gaze, avoiding the sight of her pulling the robe to cover her thighs. She was lying still and seemed to be relaxed when he looked at her again.

He renewed the veneer of clinical detachment he'd lost when examining her in her bathroom, settled her arm in the medical analysis unit, and brought the scanner above her. With a poke and pinch blood and tissue samples were taken from her arm.

"That's the worst of it."

Darcelle turned her head and smiled at him, looking him straight in the eyes. An electric shock ran through him. He snatched his gaze away, overwhelmed and yet energized at the same time and unable to form coherent thoughts. Escape. He had to get away from her, or he would step over the line he'd intentionally drawn between them. But fleeing would be idiotic. *Get a grip.* If he stood at the head of the med bed, she wouldn't be able to flash that expressive gaze at him. He forced himself to move in unhurried, steady steps, fumbling through his mental to-do list to arrive at a solution for filling the silence that hung between them. Observation test. He was planning to do that later, but it could be accomplished now.

In a brusque tone he asked, "How many statuettes are in the hallway of mirrors leading to my private apartment?" He watched her reaction.

She furrowed, then relaxed her brow. "Ten."

"What animal does the third on the left depict?"

A smirk crossed her lips. "It wasn't an animal. It's Mercury—or his head and shoulders—copied from the relief by Artus Quellinus in the Amsterdam Royal Palace on Earth. If the entire relief were depicted, it would include a rooster and a goat at his feet."

He allowed himself a small smile. "You know your Earth art history."

The scanner had moved over her face, so her response was muffled. "It was the primary focus of my undergraduate studies."

He waited for the scanner to move lower. When it did and before he could speak, she arched an eyebrow at him. "It's appropriate to have the main entrance to your private domain guarded by the god of thieves."

He chuckled. "Most people are not aware there's symbolism behind the selection."

"One out of ten."

"Exactly. The other nine statuettes have no relationship to my secret vocation. Maybe this will stump you. Are there any spots in the hallway hidden from reflection in the mirrors? Any large enough for a person to hide?"

He could tell she was trying not to smirk again. "No. The mirrors and tables are located so that the entire length of the hall is visible in at least one mirror no matter where you position yourself."

"Then it's impossible to reach the end of that hallway without being seen?"

"You might move along the ceiling, but with the vid mirrors arranged the way they are, dropping to open the door would bring you in range of the last. They are vid mirrors, I assume? For surveillance?"

"They are." This time his grin was broad. His minou had perceived more than most people untrained in situational awareness. One last question to discover how detailed her observation had been. "In the hallway, what color was the floor tile seven in and two from the left?"

She stared off in space as though she was seeing the hall in her mind's eye, and she considered for a minute. "I didn't see it. It was blocked from view by the table above it. No, I take that back. It was visible in one mirror. It was green. One of only three green tiles in the hallway. The pattern of tiles seems random. I'd have to study it longer to determine if it is."

"You have a photographic memory."

A wide grin spread across her face. "I do."

The scanner signaled that it had completed its task. "That can be useful, but it won't be enough. We'll be working on your situational awareness." He moved to stand at her side, raised the scanner, and frowned at her.

Her nose wrinkled. "I think my situational awareness is pretty good."

"Don't scowl." He dragged a finger down her forehead. "You are excellent at processing what you see, but if you had better situational awareness, I would not have been able to come up behind you when you were reading my last note. You need to be equally good using all your senses."

"Oh." She shivered when he dropped his finger to her mouth.

"That's a matter of training."

Her lips begged to be kissed. What was the harm in one kiss? He shouldn't, but the brief taste he'd had two days ago had replayed in his mind. Was it as delicious as he remembered?

"This isn't." His warm lips pressed gently against hers. When she mewled her need for more, he grinned without withdrawing from the contact, before pulling back several inches to gaze at her. "Do you want more?"

"Yes, please."

"Such pretty, imploring eyes. You could hypnotize a man with those eyes." His mouth found hers again, and this time he took the kiss deeper, penetrating her with his tongue. She skimmed her own along his, captivating him with her delectable sweetness. He was completely hooked on her taste. Fingers gripping the sides of her chin, he held her in place as though she might escape him. *Not a chance.*

The need for air made him break the kiss and pull away to look at her. Passion suffused him, but it wasn't mere physical lust. Something fiercer claimed him, threatening to vanquish his control.

The next words she whispered nearly undid him. "I want you, Matou."

"Matou?"

Her smile was shy. "That's what I named you when you first left me messages. Tomcat. Cat Burglar. It fit you, or as I imagined you to be."

"I like it. You may call me Matou." He released her arm from the medical analysis unit, scooped her into his arms, and strode with her across the gym floor. "You know what tomcat's do best?" He grinned seductively at her. "They mate with female cats."

Darcelle's response might have been humorous but for the serious expression on her face. "It's a good thing I'm here."

Gods, she was so lovely. "Huh. Yes. It's a very good thing." Rather than take the stairs up to his living space, he passed it by, stopping before an incline arm machine. He moved her from his arms to the seat, helping her lie back before securing each wrist in the arm extensions. The sash to her silk robe loosened, and the robe slipped open. He pulled it wider, his gaze roving over her as though, despite his previous clinical examination, he had never seen her nude. "You are stunning, minou."

Her tongue swept her lips, and his control broke. With an efficiency of effort he stripped his clothes, took her feet in his palms, and levered her legs up to her chest. He straddled the end of the bench seat, snugging his erection tight against her core. Bathed in the heat of both their bodies, he lowered his mouth to hers, renewing their kiss. The gentleness he'd first used with her was gone. The rampant need inside him to possess her, to claim this woman he had desired for over a year, was a violent force driving him to wild abandon.

Her response was equally fierce. Did she need him as much as he needed her? Did she want him as much as he wanted her? It didn't matter. She was his. Now. Forever. She had no choice because nothing was more essential to him than keeping this passionate woman with him always.

He wanted to melt into her, but to do that he had to be inside her. His shaft was a throbbing steel rod, and his balls were heavy. Grinding his length along her soft wetness had coated him in her juices. With a flick of his fingers, he positioned himself and surged into her. The moan that rose from deep within him mingled with her accompanying sounds of appreciation.

"Oh gods, Matou. You feel so…"

But he was past words, too deeply surrendered to the thrust and pull, the intense pleasure of the emotional and physical bond they were forging. He'd planned to give her multiple orgasms before the first time he took her, but that was no longer a certainty or even a possibility if it depended on his restraint. The base of his spine tingled, and his balls drew up. The orgasm struck him in strong throbbing waves. Buried deep inside her, he spent himself in mind-shattering pulses, ending unable to move. Ecstasy hit her, and she clamped tightly on his softening erection, squeezing out whatever fluid remained.

A trickle of sweat escaped from between their bodies. He was crushing her, so he eased back and stroked her cheek with the backs of his fingers. "Minou, my sweet wildcat. I'm sorry. I shouldn't have forced myself on you like this."

An expression crossed her face that he couldn't interpret. "You did not force yourself. I wanted you as much as you wanted me."

He brushed a fluff of her curls out of her eyes. "I was not gentle with you."

Her attempt to reach out to him was halted by the restraints on her wrists. She relaxed against the bench. "And if you had not cuffed me, you would now be covered in scratches from my nails. Are you into bondage?"

He chuckled. "No. Not really. Sometimes. I couldn't resist keeping you splayed out before me. You were quite... fetching." The press and seal closures on the machine's arm extensions helped the person exercising maintain proper position. She could have broken free with a sharp forward thrust, but either she didn't understand how the cuffs worked—not likely—or she'd chosen to stay locked in his control. Sebastian's chest lightened. Maybe this hadn't been a mistake. Perhaps she wanted to be dominated as much as he needed to control.

With a snap, both restraints released and Darcelle encircled his neck with her arms. She knew how to free herself. Sebastian grinned, welcoming the electrical tingle that shot through him when she fixed her hypnotizing gaze on his. "You are the greatest treasure I've ever stolen."

One eyebrow arched delicately, and the tingle became a zap. "You didn't steal me."

"Didn't I?"

She smirked. "No, I stole you."

"Hmmm." Did she perceive that she had hit the mark with that statement? She had stolen his notice, then his attention, and now she was stealing his heart. He'd kept that organ locked up tight under strict security. Many had tried to make him fall in love, but none had succeeded until this little kitty, his minou, had managed it without even trying. Like a cat burglar, she had crept into his life on quiet feet, slipping past his safeguards. As a thief himself, he could return the favor, because he wouldn't allow her to evade him.

He stood up and held out a hand to her. "Come. This wasn't part of the plan. You still have time to shower and dress before I introduce you to your training team."

Fingers lightly placed in his palm, she accepted his help. Deftly he tied the sash of her robe closed. He offered her his arm when he finished dressing. She smiled up at him, allowing him to escort her up the stairs. He left her at her door much to his regret. Showering with her was tempting, but he needed to speak to Max, the man who would oversee all aspects of her training. Darcelle had bitten her lip when it became apparent he wasn't coming into her room. She'd survive the disappointment. He sighed. His plan had been to monitor her progress in person. She wouldn't be pleased with him for stepping back from training her personally, but for his own sake it was necessary. For Jeanne and Cheyenne's sake, it was imperative. The focus had to be on readying her for what he thought of as the mission. Bedding her was a superfluous expenditure of time and energy.

$$* \quad * \quad * \quad *$$

IF HER INNER CAT had been bleating brief purrs of satisfaction before, it was on full rumble now. Matou had taken her to heaven. The hold she had on his muscular arm was light, but even without being skin to skin, the contact sent a current of desire through her. Oh yes. She wanted more, and the shower awaited. The two of them. Naked. Soaping each other. Licking. Sucking. Round number two couldn't begin soon enough for her.

He stopped outside her room and drew his arm from her. Once he opened the door... but he didn't. Instead he avoided eye contact with her, his eyebrows pinched together. "I'll collect you in twenty minutes. Wear something you can exercise in."

"Umm. Okay. I'll be ready." She bit her lip and tried to puzzle out the disconnect. Apparently they weren't equally affected by what had happened between them. What had happened? Sex or something more? It had seemed like something more to her, but for him it must have been just sex.

And now he was turning and walking down the hall as calm, cool, and collected as could be. Not fair. He'd mastered the three *c*'s while she was failing miserably. She thrust her shoulders back, her wounded dignity gathered around her like a shawl, entered her room, and resolved to regain her self-control.

The twenty minutes he'd allotted would go by fast, so she rushed to remove her clothes. With one longing look at the huge tub, she slipped into the shower and washed away the evidence that she had finally been with Matou. When the soap bubbles swirled down the drain, so too did her hope that he would want their relationship to move beyond a partnership of thieves.

His statement that she was the greatest treasure he had ever stolen was only words. In the throes of passion, he was a smooth talker, a real tomcat who took his pleasure where he found it. He could look elsewhere from now on. He may be sex on a stick, but she wouldn't risk her heart being broken for a roll between the sheets no matter how good he'd proven himself. Gods, he'd confirmed her explicit imaginings to the last detail and then surpassed them.

He was as physically close to perfection as any man could be. Muscles. Warm taut skin. Firm, slender fingers, experienced in the art of holding and caressing. She hadn't been able to touch his shaft with her hands, but even it had been flawless, longer than average, the girth wider, and straight as an arrow. When he'd shot into her, she'd lost herself to pure bliss. Even the scar that marred his right shoulder didn't detract from his overall appeal. Like the lock of hair that wouldn't stay in place over his left eyebrow, the scar enhanced his looks.

Water spattered when she slapped her palm against the shower wall. *Stop it! No more thinking like that.* With brisk movements she turned off the tap, exited the shower, and rubbed herself dry with the thick bath towel hanging close by. She strode through to the closet, where she grabbed a pair of workout pants, a T-shirt, and a sports bra and panties set. In her bedroom she pulled on the clothes.

Shoes. She forgot shoes. *Damn it all to hell.* Barefoot, she stomped back and found athletic shoes and socks. The mattress bounced beneath her when she sat to pull them on.

Five minutes remained before he'd come for her. Sitting around waiting would give her too much time for her thoughts to stray in directions she'd forbidden herself. She flopped backward on the bed. Gods, what had she been thinking to come here? Why had she allowed her attraction to Matou to influence her decision? Because she wanted him. Because he was different from any other man she'd ever met. Beyond handsome, yes, but something else. She couldn't define it. Not yet. But his magnetic appeal fascinated her.

She'd told him he hadn't stolen her, that the reverse was true. Maybe it wasn't true so far, but it sure as hell could be. How would he like it if she stole his heart only to reject him and walk away? Not any better than she had, she'd bet. Time for him to take a dose of his own medicine. She may not be the stellar cat burglar that Matou was, but he'd promised to train her. And while he trained her, she'd do what he least expected. He'd let a thief into his life, and she intended to do what thieves did best, robbing him of the three *c*'s while she purloined his heart. Let's see how calm, cool, and collected he was after she finished with him.

If he noticed the grin she was wearing, he'd be having second thoughts. But she wiped it away before she opened the door to his knock.

"Ready?"

"Yes." This time he didn't offer her his arm.

Side by side they walked to the dining room, not speaking to one another. Around a long, sleek, dark table, four people sat. Their gazes were assessing.

"This is Darcelle." Matou gestured to the man lounging in the chair closest to her. "Darcelle, Cade. He'll be handling your surveillance and situational awareness training."

Cade's nod of greeting was neutral. Despite his relaxed posture, he looked like a large tawny lion capable of springing at her without warning. Darcelle pulled her gaze from Cade's bland stare when Matou motioned to the woman sitting beside Cade.

"This is Bassinae. She's a fitness coach. You'll spend part of every day with her. She'll also oversee your diet."

Bassinae's short dreads bounced when she smiled and waved at Darcelle. "Hi. You appear fit, so we'll be taking you to the next level."

Darcelle returned the smile. "Sounds good."

The older man at the end of the table resembled the martial arts trainer, Master Ken Ito-Jones, who had been sent to prepare her sister for a vid role. This man was taller, without an ounce of fat, and had the direct gaze of a drill instructor. Without waiting for an introduction, the man said, "I'm Max. I'll be overseeing your training. If you have problems with anything, come to me. I'll do what I can to make things right." His expression seemed positive compared to Cade's, but Darcelle could tell he hadn't made up his mind about her yet.

"Max will also be responsible for improving your climbing, jumping, and gymnastic skills," Matou said. He pointed to the second woman seated on the far side of the table. "And this is Jeanne, my sister. She'll be showing you how to use state-of-the-art tech gear."

The woman grimaced and ran a hand through her unkempt spiky hair. "Hey."

Jeanne's unfriendly expression was unexpected, but Darcelle didn't have time to dwell on it. Matou pointed to the seat next to Jeanne. "Sit there."

After he had seated himself at the end of the table, a pair of servers appeared carrying trays. A plate with a large salad of mixed greens and a variety of chopped veggies was placed before her. The aroma of the dressing was enticing. Her stomach growled. Nerves had kept her from eating breakfast. She waited for the others to be served and for Matou to eat before she picked up her fork and dug in. Tart flavor burst across her tongue when she bit into a peewee tomato. She continued taking bites while the others conversed.

"Is everything arranged as I requested?" Matou's question was directed at Max.

"Yes, Sir. I've taken care of the details. The staff know they are not to interact with Ms. Lebeau during her training. One of us will be with her always unless she is alone in her room. The tech dampers are working."

Darcelle jerked her head to look at Matou. What? The staff wasn't allowed to talk with her? This group of people were to be her minders? And tech dampers meant she couldn't comm without asking for permission.

"Excellent." Matou reached out to pat her hand. "I said I would be in control of your life, and I meant it. These measures are not punitive. You will need to focus your entire attention on your training. No distractions."

Why, you condescending bastard! Darcelle's appetite left her. She pushed the food around with her fork until the servers returned and took the plates away, rehearsing the words she'd spew at him when she had him alone again.

Matou wiped his mouth with his cloth napkin. "Minou, I'll be busy for the next week, but you are in good hands with Max and his staff. I'll check in on your progress from time to time." He stood and went to her side, pecking her on the cheek. "I'll see you this evening at dinner." And he left.

Speechless, Darcelle could only blink at him. At his end of the table Max stood.

"Today each of us will spend time with you, evaluating your current skills and abilities. You'll begin with me, then Bassinae, then Cade, and finally Jeanne. We will take supper together here in the dining room." He lifted a tablet that had been lying on the table beside him. "Your assigned readings are on this tablet, along with your daily schedule. You'll be tested over the material, so don't skip or skim."

Darcelle glared at him, biting out her response between her teeth. "Yes, sir."

As though he were unaware of her attitude, he said, "You'll be with me first." He exited the dining room without a look back.

Okay. Yes, sir. Anything you say, sir. Darcelle followed, speeding up when his long strides put distance between them.

He halted, and Darcelle nearly ran into him.

"Put this in your room and come straight to the gym."

Darcelle took the tablet he held out to the side and scurried along the hall to her room. *Goodie. My own personal drill sergeant. Well damn them all to hell. I'll show them and Matou what I'm capable of.*

CHAPTER FIVE

MAX WAS A RELENTLESS taskmaster. When they arrived on the gym floor, Darcelle tipped her head back to look up a length of heavy rope. It dangled from the ceiling in the center of the gym's open space. A rope ladder hung about five yards away from it. *Easy peasy.* A metal cable, resembling the one she'd used on the Jepsen Building, hung next to the wall.

"Here." Max handed her a pair of leather climbing gloves. "We'll start with the ladder. Climb to the top and down. I'll be timing you."

Darcelle didn't hesitate, leaping onto the rope three rungs from the bottom. She zipped up and back down. On the floor she placed her hands on her hips, her breathing steady and unhampered.

"Not bad. You'd make better time if you were smoother with your motions. Stop swinging your ass back and forth. It messes with your center of balance and makes you jerky. Do it again, and this time keep your butt under control."

"I'll bet you enjoyed the show."

"And I'll enjoy it all day if you don't make some improvement."

With a huff, Darcelle shook out her arms and legs, attacking the ladder in an all-out effort, certain she was going much faster.

Once she made it back to the floor, Max's comments were brief. "One second better. Do it again. Focus."

One second! That's all? Focus, he says. Damn straight. I'm gonna show him focus.

Twenty minutes later, he allowed her to take a break, handing her a bottle of water. She emptied it and sat to stretch her legs.

"The rope is next. I know you've been taught the method the boss prefers for locking the rope with your feet. I want you to take it slow the first time, so I can watch your technique."

Darcelle complied, making certain her form was perfect. She didn't want another critique about her ass screwing with her center of balance.

"Nice. Okay, we'll work on speed, but don't let your technique suffer."

Halfway up the rope, a prickle ran down her spine. Matou was watching her. This time, when she levered herself higher, she rotated. The door from the penthouse into the gym was closing. He'd been there, checking on her as he said he would.

"Hey. Keep going. No distractions."

Right. How was she supposed to ignore Matou and the reaction her body had to him? Even if one sample of what the chemistry between them could achieve was enough for him, it wasn't for her. She wanted more. More of his hands on her breasts. More of his kisses on her skin. And definitely more of him surging inside her.

Argh. First get through the training. Once she was his partner, she could seduce him at her leisure. She reached high, brought her knees up, and rewrapped the rope around her feet, pushing herself higher.

This type of climbing came naturally to Darcelle. Over the next quarter hour, she improved her speed by a few seconds. Max called a second break, so she sat on the floor eating the energy bar he offered her and drinking another bottle of water.

"You're better at this than I expected. We can practice falling today."

"Falling?"

"Boss wants you to be able to release the rope, hands and feet, and stop yourself before you hit the ground."

The snack settled like a lead ball in her belly. She'd been an apt pupil at the Ups and Downs Climbing Emporium where she'd accomplished the training Matou had insisted she take during the previous year. But the instructors had never required her to release a rope.

She didn't rush up the rope this time. Hanging high above the gym floor, she looked at Max, who watched wordlessly from below. Several minutes passed while she blew air from her lungs, searching for enough determination to relax her grip and foot lock. As expected, the moment she loosened her hold and plummeted, her stomach shoved up to the top of her chest. She grabbed the rope tight and stopped herself, proud that she had slipped only a few inches.

Max spoiled the moment by yelling at her. "Really release it and unclasp your feet this time. No sliding."

Teeth clenched tight, which was a mistake, she obeyed him and fell much farther, nearly losing contact with the rope where it slid over and under her feet. Her jaw ached from the jarring it took when she clamped her feet and tightened her grip. Why did she have to release the rope? Letting it slide through her hands worked fine with the gloves she was wearing.

After that first jolting stop, she relaxed the parts of her body that weren't actively involved in halting her descent. Somewhere along the line, her stomach quit protesting.

"Slide down the rest of the way."

On the ground Darcelle finally got the chance to ask her question. "Why do I have to do that? When am I ever going to have to release a rope and drop like that?"

"Maybe never. But circumstances change, and the boss wants you able to save yourself if the rope gets away from you. You should see him do it. He doesn't just stop the fall; he decides when to do it."

Darcelle scowled, muttering under her breath, "Apparently he doesn't care to show me his amazing abilities."

Despite his pinched expression, Max didn't ask her what she'd said. "That's enough for today. You need to get better on the rope before we start with the cable. Take a break. Use the facilities. Rehydrate. Bassinae should be here soon. Good effort."

Damn. Here she'd been thinking with relief that he hadn't asked her to fall from the cable. Tenderness in her jaw made her wince when she clenched her teeth. It would require deep digging to find the courage needed to release the cable.

The next hour was spent with Bassinae. Cheerful, tormenting Bassinae. The fitness trainer promised to go easy. Stretching and a test of the basics. The basics turned out to be planks, push-ups, squats, crunches, and lunges followed by a marathon, or what seemed like a marathon to Darcelle.

The exercises wouldn't have bothered her if she hadn't already been drilled hard by Max. Bassinae worked out alongside her, smiling, encouraging, and counting off the reps as though one hundred crunches were a breeze for abdominal muscles strained from the effort of avoiding becoming a splat on the gym floor. Not that Darcelle had come close, but there was always tomorrow. Crunches were no fun. Not like wiping the smile from Bassinae's lips would be. Even after a three-mile run, the woman wasn't winded, while Darcelle bent over sucking air.

After the laps, Bassinae led Darcelle to a massage table in the med corner of the gym and worked the worst of the kinks from Darcelle's sore muscles. The massage was the deciding factor on whether she would murder Bassinae. Hate her, yes. But Darcelle wouldn't gut the trainer. They might become friends once Darcelle got herself in better shape.

Her legs were wobbly when she eased from the table. "Thanks. That was an amazing massage."

"Nothing like it for tired, sore muscles." Bassinae patted Darcelle's back. "Lunchtime. Let's grab our salads from the kitchen and eat them on the terrace."

"Sure."

Darcelle ate her seared chicken salad, wishing for more when it was gone.

Bassinae tossed her a bagel pack. "Here; I grabbed two of these. Figured you'd need some carbs."

"Thanks."

They sat in silence munching their bagels. The view from the terrace was spectacular. It looked out over a large parkland in the center of the most elite residential area in the city. Matou was wealthy, but she already knew that.

"I'll clean up here after I show you how to get to the set. Cade should be waiting on us."

Bassinae led Darcelle back to the stairs that went down to the gym, and on through a set of double doors in the corner of one end. A long corridor and three sets of stairs brought them to a warehouse-sized room that resembled a vid soundstage. A variety of room sets lined the outer edges while the center was two stories of an outdoor city set.

Cade leaned against the wall just inside the door. "Hello, ladies."

"Hey, Cade. Have fun. I'll see you later, Darcelle."

With his arms crossed over his chest—a muscular, beefy chest—Cade tilted his head and stared at her for a moment. "I understand you have problems with situational awareness."

Darcelle didn't want to admit Matou had gotten the best of her. She rubbed the toe of her shoe on the floor.

"Not to worry. That's why I'm here to help. I'm former Special Forces with the Fed fleet. I'll bring you up to snuff."

"You don't look young enough to have retired. Why'd you quit?"

His face tightened. "That, missy, is none of your business."

"Sorry."

A tight nod was his only acknowledgment of the apology. "To start, I want to test what skill you do have. I'm going to sit over there"—he pointed toward a set—"and I want you to sneak up on me and touch the back of my head. Take your time."

"Right." *This shouldn't be hard. I can be quiet.*

He settled into an easy chair in all his leonine glory on a set that simulated a typical family room. His back turned to her, he tapped the remote on the side table next to him, turning on a noisy action vid. She waited five full minutes before creeping up on him, placing one foot in front of the other, hoping he hadn't noticed the slight squeak her shoe made on the concrete floor. Before she got within three feet of him, he swiveled, aiming a gun at her.

"How'd you hear me over the vid? I was really quiet."

He looked down his nose at her, brown eyes gloating. "You were quiet—not as much as you can be, but we'll work on that. I smelled you a long way off. Don't wear perfume or anything else that has a scent to it. Anyone with a decent sense of smell will detect you before you can get close. The same holds true for slipping past guards. If you can't hear or see them, it's still possible to use your nose to determine where they are. Smoking soothe sticks is a prime example. The odor lingers long after a person finishes. In a hot environment, body odor can give you away. Your reading will give you the details on how to avoid being stinky without drenching yourself in cologne."

"Yes, sir." *Just wait, buddy. You'll regret the superior attitude.*

"We'll work on evasion techniques tomorrow. I want to test your observational skills. Once I know your capabilities, we'll do scenarios." He pointed toward the mock street. "I want you to stand by the third door down."

"The floral shop?"

"Yeah. You're guarding the door. Your job is to spot me before I get close enough to touch you. You see me, you yell red. You hear me, you yell red. You smell me, you yell red. Got it?"

"Got it." Darcelle took position in front of the shop door. All the lights except for the one shining above the doorway went out. "Hey. That's not fair. With that light over my head, I can't see in the dark."

No response came from the opaque inkiness that hemmed her in. "Fine!" *Okay. You can do this. Keep your back to the door. Rotate your gaze. And strain your ears to hear the slightest noise. At least he didn't add a soundtrack.*

Deathly quiet racked her nerves. *Is he coming? How close is he?*

The sting of something slapping the back of her hand startled her. *What the...* Cade stood by her side, holding a riding crop and chuckling.

"Gotcha."

With her thumb Darcelle rubbed the spot he had smacked. "That wasn't fair. You set me up to fail. How am I supposed to see you when my night vision is compromised? Wouldn't I have gear to assist me?"

"Worst case scenario you won't. But since you're new to this, I'll give you a break. I'll turn the lights on dim. You'll be able to see at least halfway down the block. I'll bet you still won't catch me."

Darcelle narrowed her eyes and retorted, "Try it."

Cade was soon swallowed by the obscurity as he sauntered away. The lights turned on. He was doing what he said he'd do. She could see half a block in all directions. This time he wouldn't surprise her.

Not more than a minute passed before she felt air displaced beside her and a sting on her shoulder.

During the next half hour, he placed her in a variety of scenarios, snapping her with the riding crop each time she failed to detect him. The third time he hit the same spot on her hand, she snatched the crop from him and waved it in his face.

"I don't need a gods-be-damned sadist hitting me with a riding crop to motivate me." She held the crop by each end and tried to break it over her thigh without result. With a scream, she threw it, satisfied when it skidded under the couch in the family room set.

The angry response she expected didn't come. Instead he laughed. Not a nice you-got-me, let's-be-friends laugh. No, it was an evil snigger. But he didn't fetch the crop and use it for the rest of her session with him.

By the time Cade called an end to the torment, Darcelle thoroughly appreciated what Matou had meant when he'd said she didn't have good situational awareness. Cade gave her directions to the tech safe room where Jeanne would meet Darcelle.

When she entered the room, Jeanne told her sit, so Darcelle collapsed into one of the chairs surrounding a flat wooden table.

"I'm more than ready to get off my feet. I thought I was in good shape, but I'm exhausted after what Max, Bassinae, and Cade put me through today."

"You'll get some speed heal before supper. Just see you don't get behind on your training. Everybody pulls their own weight around here. No excuses."

Okay then. I won't make another off-task remark.

On her way to change for dinner, Darcelle contemplated the time she'd spent with Jeanne. If the woman had stuck to explaining how to use subvocal transmitters and receivers and how to tap into those used by others, Darcelle wouldn't have had any complaints. Attempts to rationalize Jeanne's behavior didn't solve the puzzle. Throughout the hour, Jeanne treated her like an imbecile, snatching things from her fingers and ridiculing her. It was baffling and annoying as hell. Jeanne was Matou's sister, so maybe the woman's animosity had something to do with that.

Could be she's overprotective of her brother. Ridiculous. Matou can take care of himself. I've never met her, so she can't be holding a grudge. Maybe she's one of those people who doesn't like strangers.

Darcelle shrugged, opening the door to her room. She'd deal with whatever she had to. Whether Jeanne liked it, Darcelle would be Matou's partner. After a quick shower she pulled on a clean pair of jeans and a shirt.

She slumped into her seat at the dining table, surprised her joints didn't creak when she did. The members of her persecution-cum-training squad looked as refreshed and fit as they had at breakfast. They'd worked her hard. Matou's chair was empty. When she moved her gaze to Max, he answered her unspoken question.

"It will be the five of us tonight."

Terrific. So much for hands-on mentoring by the master cat burglar.

Supper with the fab four was a delight she didn't need. It was difficult to decide which of them she hated most. Max had been all efficiency and brisk commands, a balls-to-the-wall drill sergeant. Bassinae was annoyingly cheerful. Although her massage skills were a definite plus in her favor. Cade was an all-around asshole. And Jeanne? If she'd had to spend much more than the allotted hour with that woman, Matou's sister or not, Darcelle would have accosted her as she had Cade. Jeanne was definitely vying for the top spot on Darcelle's list of hated training squad members.

At least my appetite is fully functional. The plate of stir-fried beef and veggies looked yummy. Darcelle dug in, relishing the robust flavor and the crunch of water chestnuts.

"Ms. Lebeau."

Darcelle looked up from her plate. Max continued to address

her as Ms. Lebeau while the others called her Darcelle. Jeanne never used her name, preferring to call her *you* instead.

"Yes, sir."

"Don't forget to do your reading. Take the test for day one after you finish. It's under the test tab."

"Yes, sir."

He narrowed his eyes at her. "Tomorrow's schedule is also on the tablet. After supper, you will go to your room and remain there until breakfast tomorrow. Be here no later than half five. Understood?"

Half five. Gods! "Yes, sir." She was too tired to react with more than that perfunctory agreement.

She finished eating and dragged herself to her bedroom. The lock made a snick after she'd closed the door. When the knob refused to turn, she discovered what she'd guessed. She was locked in her room. *Just dandy!* And Matou wasn't coming to tuck her in. Surely he wouldn't leave her training to the persecution squad for the entire month. That wasn't the deal she thought she'd struck.

She stumbled into the bathroom, shedding clothing as she went. The fuzzy jammies she'd found in her closet warmed her, but they made her sleepier as well. She'd never get through her reading and test if she lay down.

Settled into the chair at the desk built into a window niche of her room, she stared outside. The evening sky was cloudless, stars twinkling in the distance. She was higher than she'd been when she climbed the Jepson Building, so the stars weren't washed out by the city lights. That had been an exhilarating night. Thoughts of it reminded her that she was here by choice. No matter what the persecution squad threw at her, no matter whether Matou ever touched her again, she would succeed because she wanted this. Wanted to be Matou's partner. *Hell. I want him. But first I'm going to teach him a lesson.*

She had four weeks to steal his heart and break it. Would that be enough time? It had to be. Fingers fiddling with the edge of her tablet, a scene of him begging her to take him back played in her mind. If, hard as it was to imagine, he enacted the role of penitent supplicant properly, she would eventually agree to forgive him.

Her inner cat yowled in protest. The submissive part of her could shut up. Its opinion wasn't needed. She opened the tablet to read her first lesson.

CHAPTER SIX

SEBASTIAN STEPPED FROM the shower, dried off, and hastily donned a shirt and shorts for climbing. The last week had been excruciating. His focus on business hadn't been worth a counterfeit credit.

The reason for his distraction was at this moment with Max in the gym. Darcelle Lebeau. Wildcat and kitten. His minou. He hadn't been able to stop himself from watching her. Darcelle had known he was observing her. Her head would turn toward him, and a slight smirk would cross her lips. After skipping the first evening meal, he'd forced himself to attend breakfast and dinner every day. He could handle the searing desire to touch Darcelle if he allowed himself short doses of her company. Or that's what he'd told himself. It hadn't worked out that way. If anything, it ratcheted up his need.

He slapped closed the binding on his shoes and left his bedroom, his whole body vibrating with the need to be near her. He should never have had sex with her. Not if he intended to keep his distance until she decided to stay. But his decision to back off had seemed more and more arbitrary as each day passed. Eager was a pale word to describe the sensations coursing through him. He hadn't experienced this in… damn, in a very long time. Maybe not since he was a kid awaiting a rare trip to the Alien Planets Amusement Park.

When he entered the gym, his gaze met hers at once. She was hanging from the top of the metal climbing cable. The next instant she was plummeting toward the floor. His stomach fell and chest went tight. She caught herself two-thirds of the way down.

Max glared up at her and hollered, "Better. But you should never drop more than half the length of that cable before you break your fall."

Darcelle stared at Sebastian, a smile flickering on her lips. Max turned to find out what she was looking at. "Boss. You're here."

Sebastian grinned. "I am. You've made progress with your trainee."

"She's getting the hang of things." Faint praise if stated by anyone other than Max.

Darcelle used the interruption to slide to the bottom of the cable without permission. Normally Max would have scolded her for that, but while Sebastian jogged down the stairs to the gym floor, Max sent her to get a drink.

Both men lowered their voices when they met face-to-face. "She's doing better than I expected." Sebastian's gaze drifted to Darcelle where she leaned against the wall, sipping from a water bottle and staring at him. The workout clothes she wore clung to every part of her luscious body.

"She's a fast learner."

Sebastian broke his contemplation of her to focus on Max. "Will she be ready in time?"

"She's close now."

Sebastian couldn't stop himself from looking her way again. Rather than sipping, she drained the contents of the water bottle, walked to the refuse receptacle, and tossed the bottle away. The sway of her hips was undoubtedly for his benefit.

Max looked over his shoulder at Darcelle and grunted. "She's a fine-looking woman with a lot of grit."

"That she is," Sebastian said, yanking his attention away from her and clapping Max on the arm. "You've achieved more than I expected. Have you started jump training today as I asked?"

"Not yet. I knew the cable work was an essential element of your plan, so I focused on that first. The supplements she's been taking to support rapid muscle recovery and growth are working. Bassinae's been hitting hard on upper body strength. I'll tell her to start the vertical jump regimen. Ms. Lebeau already has excellent leaping ability. She came to us in good shape."

"She follows instructions well." Sebastian chuckled. "Although she's been known to reorder them to fit her own priorities." A Viking knife came to mind.

"Even with you?"

Sebastian spread his mouth in a closed-lip smile. "Yep."

"I never told you. She put Cade in his place the first day."

Sebastian crossed his arms. "Oh yeah?"

Max snorted. "He was snapping her with a riding crop whenever she screwed up. Grabbed the crop out of his hand and shook it in his face. Even tried to snap it over her knee. Called him a gods-be-damned sadist."

In a carefully controlled tone of voice Sebastian asked, "Did he stop?"

"Fuck yeah. He's half in love with her but would never show it. Some shit about earning his respect."

Sebastian's stomach hardened. "Do I need to have a talk with him?"

Max smooshed his lips. "Nah. She belongs to you, and he knows it. I can't see him crossing the line with her."

"He'd better not."

Max, hands on hips, turned to face Darcelle when she approached them. "You taking over her training now?"

"I am." Sebastian observed Darcelle sauntering toward him, regarding him with seductive eyes. How had he gone a whole week with this captivating woman in reach and not laid a finger on her?

"She's meeting Bassinae in forty-five minutes."

Sebastian's response was curt. "Right."

Darcelle stopped in front of him, hands at her sides, feet planted in a wide stance. So, his minou believed she could take him on. The sound of a door shutting registered Max's departure in the small part of his brain that wasn't immersed in the sight and aroma of Darcelle. She was wearing the perfume he'd purchased for her, a vivid blend of cardamom, vanilla, and musk, with a hint of incense.

Cade had to have taught her the danger of scent, so he must not be working on her evasion techniques.

He reached out, pulled the elastic from her ponytail, and clasped his hand around the back of her head, tunneling his fingers into her springy cinnamon-colored curls. After a moment of resistance, she allowed him to pull her toward him and up onto her toes. When his lips met hers, a sense of rightness flooded him. Her smell, her taste, the texture of her lips. A woman so perfectly suited to him had to be his. Plans of how he made that inevitable slipped from his mind while he succumbed to the pleasure of kissing Darcelle.

The distance between them was too great. He needed her closer, so he wrapped her warm, pliant body in his arms, pressing his chest against the yielding mounds of her breasts. Darcelle was a feast. He fisted his hand in her hair, making it impossible for her to pull away. Her plaintive mew finally registered, and with a groan he pulled his mouth from hers. "I missed you, Minou."

The misty gray of her eyes was a narrow rim surrounding deep black dilated pupils. She was as intoxicated by him as he was by her. He calculated he had enough time to hoist her over his shoulder, take her to her room, and ravish her.

The daydream of peeling her clothes away, of exposing her tawny bronze charms covered by the thin layer of fabric, was shattered when she glared at him. "I'm not sleeping with you again."

When he released her, she stepped back and once again planted her feet wide, smacking her fists on her hips. She smiled up at him, her expression both smug and defiant at the same time.

"Is that right?"

"I didn't come here to have a sexual relationship with you. I came here to become your partner." With one long stride she narrowed the gap between them, snatched his shirt much as he had fisted her hair, and fixed her roiling rain cloud–gray gaze on him. The air became too heavy to breathe. Was she aware that her body, a mere inch away, didn't intimidate him? His shaft was so hard it might pierce synthsteel, but he would prefer to penetrate her moist heat. Her mouth would do, but sinking into her depths was his true ambition. Was he seeing things? A streak of lightning flashed in her eyes.

"Get your mind out of my pants." She used the hand wrapped in the front of his shirt to push him, and he obliged her, falling back while grinning in a bemused manner, not meant to irritate but impossible to restrain.

The gym floor resounded with the thump of her feet when she stomped away.

"Where are you going?"

She threw her response over her shoulder. "Anywhere but here."

"You can't leave. You're in the middle of a training session."

If she'd had fur, it would be standing on end. She fairly bristled. Each word a stab of sound, she said, "I need a break. I'll be back in five." With a shove she pushed through the bathroom door, slamming it behind her.

Whatever game she was playing, it was obvious she was attracted to him. And he loved her sass. He'd been worried she'd find him too controlling, but the aggressive play she'd instigated proved she could stand up to him. She'd done the same to Cade. He'd rolled over, but Sebastian wasn't in Cade's position. *If she wants to play a game of tug-of-war, I'll win and use the rope to bind her to me.*

✳   ✳   ✳   ✳

THAT DIDN'T GO WELL. Even while she'd stomped her way toward the bathroom, Darcelle's confidence had slipped away. She slammed the door more from anger at herself than at Matou and promptly ran into the wall turning the sharp corner into the facility. *Damn it all to hell! That hurts!* Her heart was racing, and she was sweating like she did after finishing a run with Bassinae. *Calm down. Focus.* She closed her eyes and rubbed her arm where no doubt a bruise was forming.

With a huffed sigh she slumped against the wall and sank to the chilly tile floor. The strategy to seduce Matou when he finally gave her the chance had worked until he'd tugged her to him and kissed her. One kiss was all it took for her mind to go numb and her inner wanton to thwart her schemes. She'd had him, and then... *I swear his nose twitched when he caught my scent.*

She brought a hand to her forehead. Her hair was billowing around her head, and she didn't have another elastic. One more thing she couldn't control. Her plan had been simple. Seduce Matou. Make him lose his heart to her. And dump him. Pretty stupid as plans went. All she'd managed was to make him fall further in lust. After a week of avoiding her, he wanted to take back up where he'd left off. Which was perfect. Until he'd overwhelmed her with one kiss. She'd been kidding herself. A man like Matou was too sophisticated to go for a girl like her. She, on the other hand, kept falling for him like a lump of synthsteel. What should she do?

His expression when she'd said she wasn't sleeping with him again had been priceless. But it hadn't been long before a taunting smirk had played around the edges of his lips. So she'd doubled down. Grabbing him by the shirt might have been overdramatic, but when he'd pretended to feel the impact of her shove and flashed a condescending smile at her... It had been too much. She'd marched in here, and now she had to go back and train with him in a few minutes.

Maybe her reaction had been the right tack to take. Refuse his sexual overtures. That would frustrate him. And it might be more aggravating than when he'd dumped her at her door and left her hanging for a week. If he tried to kiss her, she'd bite him. She thumped her head against the wall. He'd probably enjoy that. *I'm doomed no matter what I try. I'll fall for him. Hell, I already have. He won't fall for me. My heart will be broken. Crap, crap, crap. Stop letting him control the situation. I can't have what I want, so he doesn't get what he wants.*

She stood and went to the sink to splash her face. The cool water was a relief. She plucked a white towel from the rack, scrubbed dry, and on her way out the door, dumped it in the refresher bin, squaring her shoulders.

When she reentered the gym, Matou was at the console for the climbing wall. Several panels now extended three feet out. While he continued making changes, more slid into view. Without turning to look at her, he said, "Put on the safety harness." He nudged it with his foot.

Her hair interfered with slipping the straps over her shoulders.

"Here." With brusque efficiency he tied it back with an elastic he pulled from his wrist. Her elastic. No way did he keep a hair tie on his wrist. Mr. Calm, Cool, and Collected was back. She ought to have expected him. Whenever anything the least bit emotional occurred between them, out came the three *c*'s.

Finished at the console, he brushed her hands aside and adjusted the harness tabs himself. His gaze never met hers even though she didn't let hers move from his face.

"We should talk about what happened."

He stooped to check her shoes, continuing to avoid looking at her. "Nothing to discuss. You requested our relationship remain professional. You were correct to do so." When he rose to his feet, his body skimmed along hers. She fisted her hands.

His eyelids lifted, and his gaze plunged into her. Oh gods. Those green eyes were her undoing. It wasn't a color you associated with heat, but his stare was smoldering as though it was on the precipice of bursting into flame.

"I'll have no trouble keeping my pants zipped if that's what you prefer."

With that expression? Not a chance. "Oh yeah?" She gripped his length through his shorts. "You're going to walk around like this all the time?"

The next moment, her back was pressed against the wall and her wrists held in his tight grip on either side of her face. He lowered his head and waited a beat, staring at her. The urge to lower her gaze was strong, but she refused to submit to the dominance that had rushed at her, flattening her and robbing her of breath.

His voice pitched low, he said, "Do not play games, minou. You'll lose. I will have my way with you. If not now, soon."

"Yes." Her softly squeaked response held nothing of the intensity of emotion with which she'd slipped it through her panting.

"Say that again."

This time she controlled her heaving chest enough to give her reply more force. "Yes."

When his mouth met hers, claiming her lips in as carnal a kiss as she'd ever received, everything inside her loosened. Her muscles and bones became useless. If Matou didn't have her pressed tight against the wall, she would have slumped to the ground.

Something else had released its grip on her. That interior part of her that had been railing at her to maintain her perspective and keep control of the situation had melted into the background, quiescent. She didn't miss it. Instead her inner kitty was purring so loud it wouldn't have surprised her if Matou said he could hear it.

Matou broke the kiss before she had the mental composure to respond fully to it. In a flurry of motion he released the tabs on the lower portions of her harness, yanked her pants off, and whirled her around, bending her over. He slapped each of her hands against the wall and said, "Keep them there."

She ought to be humiliated. Her naked ass was exposed for anyone who entered the gym to see. But rather than yowl a protest, she wanted him to get on with it. He smacked her bottom with his hand.

"Oh!"

"This is for the blatant attempt to seduce me." Another stinging slap landed.

If you'd asked her before this experience if being spanked by Matou would be painful and degrading, she would have said yes. But now...? Now she pressed her ass higher, seeking more. Each time his palm struck her, the pitch of her arousal rose. *I like getting spanked.* She'd sort that out later, because nothing would interfere with her enjoyment of the moment.

Instead of the next smack she was expecting, Matou plunged his shaft into her, invading her core and continuing the staccato pace he'd established with his hand. He was pure tomcat, taking her for his own pleasure, and she responded like a female cat in heat, submitting to his rock-hard need to assuage her own inner lust for his hot seed.

With one hand on her hip and the other playing with her nipple, Matou pounded his way to completion. He ground deep into her and held himself there until his body shuddered. And she came around him with her own hard spasms of ecstasy.

Still holding her, he swung her and slumped to the floor, his back against the wall. Every bit of her body was sublimely relaxed. She could stay nestled between his legs, resting against him forever.

She wasn't sure how long they sat, panting, waiting for their bodies to return to normal. Matou skimmed his fingers along her skin. Before she was ready to stand, he pulled her to her feet, scooped her in his arms, and carried her to the bathroom.

Plunked on the vanity counter, Darcelle watched while Matou ministered to her. He spread her legs and cleaned away the evidence of his climax.

"Thank you."

Without a word he took her face between his hands. His gaze this time was penetrating, as though he was peering into her depths, trying to comprehend what motivated her.

"I was afraid."

His eyes narrowed. "Afraid of me?"

"No. You want to control me. Part of me wanted that, and it scared me."

"And now?"

She dropped her chin. With a gentle finger he lifted her head. "Look at me."

When she did, his need to compel her to submit to his will was visible in the tension in his jaw despite the calm expression he struggled to layer over that desire. "I've decided to not let fear keep me from whatever we might have together."

For a moment he stared into her eyes, furrowing his brow. "It's my nature to take charge of everything and everyone around me. To do otherwise makes me uncomfortable, but if we are to become the partners I hope for, trust must be reciprocal. I'm willing to cede some of my control, if you're willing to rely on me to lead. Understand. I will take care of you, but if I overstep, you must tell me so. Can you do that?"

Her smile broadened from a glimmer while he spoke. "Yes." To emphasize her answer, she placed a hand on his cheek, stroking his skin lightly with her fingertips. "And in the bedroom? If we ever get there?"

With a growl, he kissed her. "In the bedroom I'm in charge. Completely. Totally. Without exception."

A grin replaced his scowl when she giggled and said, "Absolutely!"

"We need to get to your training." He slapped her on the thigh and helped her off the counter.

"Let me put my shorts back on."

"Yes, do that or we'll never get anything accomplished."

On the way out the bathroom door, she giggled again.

CHAPTER SEVEN

SEBASTIAN WATCHED Darcelle while she gracefully maneuvered through the obstacle course he'd arranged for her. She was remarkable. In the two weeks since they'd come to their understanding, he'd split his time between business and Darcelle. Early mornings, she trained with him. After a mutually pleasurable shower and breakfast together, he went to his office, and she stayed behind to work with Max, Cade, and Bassinae. Jeanne had declared Darcelle proficient at assembling and using the tech gear available to them.

Darcelle had appeared pleased to be spared regular time with Jeanne. For a reason he couldn't fathom, his sister didn't get along with Darcelle. From what he could see, Darcelle wasn't provoking Jeanne. At breakfast and dinner Darcelle never responded to Jeanne's digs with animosity, unlike the comebacks she flung at Cade. Which Cade enjoyed. The two had settled into a caustic if friendly rivalry. Jeanne hadn't moved an inch toward accepting Darcelle. When the time came, she would have to set aside her hostility for the mission he had planned. Jeanne had the most to lose if they failed. Maybe that was the root of her antagonism of Darcelle. *I'll have to talk to her.*

Tomorrow he intended to lay his plans before the group to prepare for and practice different elements of the job. That he could begin a week early pleased him. He would tell Darcelle tomorrow that she had passed her initial one-month training period in record time. Twenty-one days instead of thirty.

The sound of her triumphant *yes* when she made the last tricky leap brought a smile to his lips. He'd been smiling more lately, and she was the reason for it. His minou.

It had been a risk, telling her he wouldn't control every part of her life. Even while he'd said the words, he'd appreciated that it would take effort not to treat her like a member of his staff. He'd had girlfriends in the past, but their primary complaint had been that exact point. They were no better than his cook, just providing a different service. But he wanted more from his relationship with Darcelle. So he'd fought his nature and allowed her more leeway than he'd given any woman before.

None of those women had remained indelibly imprinted on his mind for a year, a year in which he'd never touched her or spoken to her in person. He'd watched her, written notes to her, and enjoyed her unique methods of handling his assignments. She was like no other woman. Once he'd caressed her, kissed her, made love to her, it had become impossible to let her go.

So here he stood, watching a woman who had gradually taken over most of his waking thoughts, and rather than bridling at the restriction, he was enjoying it. She brightened his life. And he was drifting toward trusting her, enough so that ceding a greater measure of control over their relationship and his personal life to her was getting easier. A kernel of doubt niggled at him. *No, call it what it is...fear.* He'd promised her the choice of deciding whether to stay. If her response to his lovemaking last night were any predictor, she would. And he believed that. But still...what if she didn't? He'd cleared his schedule. When he told her the good news, he'd request an immediate decision. No more time to consider. *If she hasn't decided what she wants by now—*

His internal comm pinged. It had to be Max or his primary assistant. No one else would interrupt him while he was training Darcelle. "Play message."

It was Max, informing him he had a visitor, Cassie, and she said it was urgent. Damn. She was not supposed to be here. If Darcelle saw her... He commed Cade and asked him to take over Darcelle's training. When Cade arrived, Darcelle was completing her third run through the course. She sauntered toward him, a spring in her step.

"Minou, Cade will take over. Something has come up that I need to deal with."

Darcelle grinned at Cade. "No problem. Maybe Cade would like to try the course. See how he compares with me."

Cade scowled at the taunt, and Sebastian left them to hash out their rivalry.

When Sebastian entered the small sitting room off the entry foyer, Cassie was standing looking at a painting. Every part of her was glamorous, from the clothing she wore to the studied perfection of her posture. Despite being Darcelle's identical twin, the sisters looked nothing alike. Where Darcelle was energetic motion, Cassie was languid. Darcelle was lousy at hiding her emotions, while you couldn't always determine Cassie's feelings.

In a few brisk strides he arrived at Cassie's side. She continued to inspect the Picasso replica for a moment before turning to him. A wide smile brightened what had been a pensive expression. "Darling. You look wonderful. Life with my sister agrees with you. I'm so glad I brought her to your attention."

"Tell me you didn't come here to check on her. We agreed you should stay away until I'd settled things with her."

"Oh, don't scowl at me like that. I wouldn't have come if I hadn't thought it important." She strolled to a side table and, with a distracted air, picked up the porcelain figurine standing on it. "There's been a small...I'm not sure what to call it...mistake made." She focused her gaze on the statuette, studying it carefully.

"A mistake?"

"Good gods, Sebastian. This is a man...he's..."

"Wanking, fapping, beating his meat, self-pleasuring..."

She returned the figurine with a clink. "Masturbating. How like you to have pornographic artworks in your receiving room."

Cassie was a woman who could and did play games. It was second nature to her. "Come now. We both know you're not a prude. Drop the role."

Smile sharp, she crossed her arms over her chest. "All right. Desmond screwed up. He's not made for intrigue. Secrets spill out of him. And he makes things worse by going stiff and wide-eyed likes he's been caught being naughty. He's such a dear. Why only yesterday—"

"Get to the point."

She tilted her head and batted her eyes. "Always in such a hurry."

"Cassie."

Lips pursed into a pretty pout, she wrinkled her nose at him. "Okay. I'll tell you. Desmond gave the game away while my mother was visiting today."

"What did he say?"

"Something about Darcelle being with you. My mother latched on to that and coaxed out every detail Desmond knew. Which weren't many. Thank goodness. I was afraid he might spill the beans to Mother. You were right not to confide in him your plan to help Jeanne. He would have wanted to assist and would have given the whole thing away. Especially since we see some of the Westeens socially."

Sebastian combed his fingers through his hair. "What will your mother do?"

"She's going to come over here and find out for herself, going to rescue Darcelle and bring her back to the bosom of her family." Cassie unfolded her arms and waved a hand in the air. "Something about putting her back on the path of her destiny. I don't know why Mother insists I use Darcelle as my personal assistant. She's not suited for it at all. Makes mistakes I have to ignore because she's family. If it weren't for Desmond, I wouldn't even be here. He insisted I come tell you."

"How altruistic of you."

"Yes. Well. I've beaten Mother here by thirty minutes at most. Desmond is stalling her. She'll figure out he knows nothing of real interest and be over here as soon as she does."

"I see. Thank you for the warning. Why didn't you comm me?"

Cassie strolled toward him and patted his cheek. "Oh darling. I intend to be here when the fireworks explode. You. My mother. This should be epic." With a smirk on her face, Cassie smoothed her palms over his shoulders and adjusted the collar of his shirt. "There. Ruffled feathers back in place. I'm staying."

"Fine." Sebastian rubbed his neck. *I'll have to move up my timetable. Tell Darcelle her thirty days ended early and get her answer to whether she intends to stay with me. By the time her mother arrives, we'll be a committed couple. And I can circumvent her mother's harangue.*

✳　✳　✳　✳

GETTING CADE TO attempt the course had been easy. Darcelle had compared his abilities to her own in a negative light, and his competitive alpha nature had done the rest. Once he was out of sight, she'd left to follow Matou. She giggled to herself. Unbelievable. Matou had turned her into a giggly girl. She'd do more than giggle when she surprised him. Her stealth skills were nearly on par with Cade's now. Well…closer.

His office was empty. Where had he gone? She heard Max moving around in the stockroom at the end of the hall. Several boxes were stacked in the center on a pallet, and Max was shelving the contents. When he noticed her, he said, "Can I help you?"

"Do you know where Sebastian is?"

Max scowled at her. "He has a guest. It's private. You should be with Cade."

"Sorry. I didn't realize he was doing something confidential. I can wait."

"Good." Max stood watching her and, when she didn't leave at once, said, "Scoot."

So she scooted, but not back to Cade and the obstacle course. Her curiosity was aroused. She wouldn't spy on him. Not really. But a glimpse his visitor couldn't hurt. No eavesdropping. Where would he meet a guest? Somewhere near the entry foyer if he didn't bring them to his office. Or maybe the living room. She'd pass it on the way to the main entrance, so she'd try there first.

Darcelle eased along the faux-steel paneled hallway that ended at the doorway into the living room. The room was silent. A quick peek past the threshold proved it was empty. She shook her arms, loosening tight muscles before moving with quiet, even steps toward the reception rooms that awaited guests at the front of the apartment.

Voices could be heard coming from the smaller of the two receiving rooms. She froze, silently listening. It was impossible to distinguish what they were saying, but the deeper voice was Matou, and his guest was female. The slender slice of guilt nagging at her disappeared. She couldn't resist finding out more. Perhaps a hint of jealousy was assailing her. This was someone he knew, someone comfortable dropping in on him.

After a pause to steel her nerves, she looked around the edge of the door and caught a brief glimpse before she recoiled. *What the hell is Cassie doing here? And why is she touching Matou?*

Hands fisted, she swept into the room. "Look who's here. I don't remember issuing an invitation, Cassie. How'd you find me? Nose in the air sniffing? No? Felt the need to drop in on a friend?" Darcelle turned her glare on Matou. "I hope I haven't interrupted something important."

Sebastian removed Cassie's hand, which she had placed on his shoulder, and went to Darcelle. He took hold of her fists, rubbing his thumb to get her to open them, and when she did, he brought their joined hands to his chest. "Your sister came to warn me your mother is coming here."

Over his shoulder Cassie was examining the ornaments on the mantel. As though she knew Darcelle was looking at her, Cassie aimed a satisfied glance her way.

Bitch. It's just like Cassie to screw with my life. Charming every man she meets. Not that Matou seemed to enjoy her touching him. Still.

Matou thwarted Darcelle's attempt to pull her hands from his. The deep breath she took filled her nose with his scent—citrus, leather, charcoal, and Matou himself. A memory of his taste when he kissed her, a hint of spices and something a tinge bitter, roused an unwanted lust within her. Gods! Her own body was betraying her.

"Darcelle—"

"No. I speak first. You are a—"

With a firm but not painful grip, Matou took her by the upper arms and pulled her toward a chair.

"Get your hands off—"

Before she could finish, he plunked her into it and turned to drag a coffee table in front of it.

A single word from Cassie punctuated his actions. "Goodness."

Sitting on the low table allowed Sebastian to stare directly into Darcelle's eyes. She straightened, crossed one leg over the other, knocking the toe of her shoe against his shin, and rested her fingertips on the arms of the chair.

They both spoke at the same time, Darcelle excoriating him for not mentioning that he knew her sister before what he was saying registered on her brain. "What did you say?"

"I said, my name is Sebastian St. Croix. My brother, Desmond, is your sister, Cassie's, boyfriend."

Darcelle uncrossed her legs and clasped her hands in her lap. "Not that part. The other. You want me to stay and be your girlfriend?"

His nostrils flared. "Yes." He closed his eyes for a moment before opening them and releasing the breath he'd held through his nose.

"You're angry with me."

He leaned in and her heart thudded. "No. I'm not angry with you. At the situation, yes. But you, no." Emotion choked his voice.

"This is a touching scene, but Mother will be here soon," Cassie said.

"Shut up!" Darcelle was gratified by the shocked expression on Cassie's face.

"Minou, I need you to believe, I will never use you like your mother and sister have. They treat you like you are worthless, barely good enough to be an unpaid personal assistant to further your sister's cinematic career. You're a nonentity to them, and it infuriates me. No one with your obvious talent and exceptional mind should be subjugated to such a role by her own family. I admit, I'm a controlling SOB, but I will cherish you every moment you are with me. Please stay." He reached out to touch her hand but pulled back before his fingers met hers. "Stay with me."

Darcelle had never seen Matou in anything but full command of a situation. He'd stepped out of that role, giving her a true choice, not one laden with expectations or coercive enticements. He'd laid his heart before her, offering her the chance to stomp on it or clasp it to her to protect. Breaking it had been her plan an eternity ago. They were long past such juvenile plotting. He loved her. His willingness to be vulnerable to her was a gift.

"I'm so sorry for doubting you." Darcelle leaped forward, clasping him around the neck, overbalancing him. They landed in a heap on the coffee table with their heads hanging off the edge.

Matou held her in a tight embrace. "This is uncomfortable."

"Yes."

"Hang on." He rolled them sideways, off the table and onto the thick carpet, catching himself on his forearms so he didn't land on her. Transfixed by his solemn expression, Darcelle stared into eyes that seemed to plumb her depths.

"Will you stay with me, Darcelle Lebeau, and be my love?"

"Yes, Sebastian St. Croix. I will."

A wide grin spread across his face. He claimed her mouth, his kiss instantly hot, deep, and demanding. Arousal blazed through her like a wildfire. Matou was hers. All hers. Only the need for a fresh lungful of air prompted them to pause.

"Ahem. Still here." Cassie's voice dripped with cynicism. "If Mother finds him on top of you like that, darling Sister, she'll be threatening legal action. I can see it now. Disgustingly wealthy businessman holds mentally defective woman hostage to use in sexually deviant ways. Mother sues for custody of daughter, demanding a billion credits in damages."

From the doorway came the sound of a throat being cleared.

Without moving his gaze from Darcelle, Sebastian snarled. "What?"

"A Ms. Lebeau is coming up in the lift."

"Thank you, Max. Please escort her here."

He scooped Darcelle's face between his hands and kissed her, holding nothing back. If the heat and strength of his body hadn't anchored her to the here and now, she would have floated in a cloud of happiness, unaware that real life was fast approaching.

But she didn't have the luxury of drifting in a haze of bliss. Dear gods, her mother was coming.

With Matou's help she stood and straightened her clothes. When she attempted to bring her hair under control, Matou stopped her. "Don't. I like it this way, wild and free."

"All right. But you need a little primping." She smoothed his hair in place with her fingers, arranging the errant lock of hair on his forehead. "Perfect."

Cassie snickered but didn't leave her spot by the mantel.

The click of her stylish boots preceding her, Darcelle's mother stalked into the room. Her hair was trimmed so short it was impossible to detect the tight curls her dark features suggested it should have. Even without the vibrant red, white, and black of the color-blocked pantsuit she wore, no one would miss the woman's entrance. She brushed past Sebastian, who had stepped forward to greet her, aiming straight for Darcelle.

"I've come to take you with me. Get your things. We are leaving here as soon as possible. If I'd known you'd fallen into the hands of this…this man"—she glared at Sebastian—"I would have come sooner. I knew something like this was bound to happen. I should never have allowed you to go out on your own. It was too much—"

From previous confrontations Darcelle knew it was best to let her mother vent some steam before injecting a rebuttal amid the outburst. But this time with Sebastian there to witness the humiliating way her mother treated her, Darcelle was seconds away from launching her own tirade.

Sebastian interposed his body between the two women. "We haven't met, madam. I am Sebastian St. Croix. I understand that you are concerned for your daughter."

Darcelle's mother took a step closer and shook her finger at Sebastian. "I'm more than concerned. Your own brother has been telling me you've enticed my daughter into becoming your partner. That you are training her in some kind of activities. I don't know what. Desmond couldn't even name them. But I can imagine, and I will not allow you to take advantage of her. You should be ashamed of exploiting such a naive young girl. I know all about men like you. Think you own the world and everyone in it. Well my daughter will not be taking part in any more of your depraved activities, whatever they may be."

"I thought you didn't tell Desmond." Sebastian threw the statement and a glare Cassie's way.

With a shrug Cassie said, "I might have said a little more than I should have."

Like a bulldog, Darcelle's mother rounded on her. "I told you to get your things. Don't stand there like you have a choice in the matter. It's fortunate I learned about this"—she waved her hands in the air—"den of iniquity before you came to any real harm. I warned you nothing good would come of moving out of your family home. Now you realize you should have listened to me.

"Cassandra, I don't know why you are here, but you can at least make yourself useful. Go help your sister pack her things."

"Me? You want me to help her pack?"

Darcelle's mother threw her hands over her head. "Why must I endure so much grief from my children?" She latched on to Darcelle's arm and tugged. "Fine. Show me where your clothes are. I'll help you pack."

With her heels dug in, Darcelle refused to budge. "Mother! I'm not leaving."

"You most certainly are. I've had enough of this independence nonsense. It's perfectly clear you can't be on your own. You're lucky I'm here to take up the reins once again."

"Mother! I'm not a horse that needs to be harnessed and told where to go. Neither was I born to pull you and Cassie around. I'm a grown woman. I've built my own life. I will not now, nor will I ever return to the way things used to be. If you and Cassie want to be a part of my life, you will accept me on those terms. If not, I will never see or speak to you again. Now get the hell out!"

For the first time Darcelle could remember, her mother was speechless. Her cheeks had gone slack, and her chin trembled.

"I…I…" She turned her head as though searching the room. "Come, Cassandra. I know when I'm not wanted."

"Yes, Mother." Cassie came and took her mother by the arm, patting her and murmuring soothing words. At the doorway to the room, Cassie looked back. "You didn't have to be so harsh, but don't worry. She'll get over this. We're family, after all." She steered her mother out into the hallway, where the wailing began. It was a relief when the penthouse entrance closed behind them.

Sebastian wrapped Darcelle in his arms. "Are you okay?"

"I'm fine." Darcelle snuggled into him.

"You were hot. Telling your mother off."

"I *was* angry."

"The other kind." He tipped her chin up and kissed her, long and slow, an invitation to more.

"Oh. Really?"

"Yeah."

After another thorough kiss, he said, "How about a bubble bath? Wash away all the ick."

"You too?"

"I like bubbles."

"You like bubbles?"

He popped her bottom with his palm. "Sure. If there's a fiercely sexy woman underneath them."

CHAPTER EIGHT

DARCELLE GAZED FROM under half-open eyelids at Matou. He slept, black hair disheveled, face made roguish by a dark stubble of beard, his lips parted. One muscled arm was slung across her chest. Her Matou. Or should she call him Sebastian? No, he was her Matou as she was his minou. Her tomcat. His kitty.

The moment Cassie and her mother had left, Matou had lifted her in his arms and carried her to his bedroom. In the bathroom he filled his sunken tub with sudsy hot water, peeled her clothes off, and gently settled her into the bubbles. After climbing in and settling himself, he pulled her on top. His eyes had been riveted on her breasts, so she exaggerated the rhythm of her body's motion, ensuring that the bubbles streamed from them, exposing the tips of her nipples each time she arched her back. It hadn't taken much of that for him to seize control of the pace. She smiled in satisfaction at the memory.

They'd spent the rest of the day and parts of the night making love, with breaks to eat from the food Matou ordered or to sleep wrapped in each other's arms. She lifted her head a moment to check whether her fingernails had left marks on his back. Pinned under his arm, she couldn't get a good look but was certain he hadn't come through the night unscathed. At one point he'd leisurely used his lips, tongue, and fingers to explore every part of her. A shiver ran through her.

Matou pressed his hand into her side and pulled her closer to him.

Once again focusing her gaze on him, she reciprocated by stroking his ass, his very fine ass, and observing his face. His eyelashes fluttered. His penetrating eyes, the palest shade of green she'd ever seen, were studying her right back.

"Good morning, minou."

"Good morning."

"Gods, even with morning breath I want to kiss you."

Darcelle pulled her arm out from under him and covered her mouth. "Oh. Sorry."

He grinned, rolled to his side and drew her arm down. When his lips met hers, she tried to keep her own sealed, but he pressed his tongue along the seam until she relented and opened to him. By the time he ended the kiss, her core had heated, and she was undulating against him. In a husky voice she said, "That was nice even though your breath is worse than mine."

His eyes widened. "Worse? My breath is worse?" He levered himself on top of her, pinning her arms over her head.

She couldn't help the smirk. "Definitely worse."

"We'll see about that." He nuzzled his face into her neck. Instead of the nibble she was expecting, he blew a raspberry and applied more liberally to every spot of skin he could reach while resisting her attempts to free herself from his grip. She finally dissolved into giggles when the effort proved futile.

He brought his head up, a silly grin on his face. This playful Matou was an unexpected delight. Who would have believed this sophisticated, elegant man had a taste for childish frivolity? Few would ever witness this side of him. His siblings, mother, and now her. He'd let her in deeper than the other women he'd slept with. Bassinae had explained Matou's love life pre-Darcelle. No woman ever stayed around long. And he never took them into his own bed. When Darcelle had asked how Bassinae knew this, the fitness trainer had raised her eyebrows, dropped her chin, and given Darcelle a look that questioned Darcelle's intelligence. The servants. Obvious when she thought about it. But now he was hers, and she would do whatever it took to keep him.

His lightheartedness transformed into an intensity that crackled with authority. "You are so beautiful, minou. Irresistible."

With a nudge of his knee he pushed her leg wider and was in her in one deep thrust, his lips claiming hers, a supreme example of his ability to control her mind and body when she was beneath him. He was a drug that increased its addicting power the more she imbibed him.

Fingernails embedded in the skin of his perfect ass, she tried to increase the maddening tempo of his slow plunge and withdrawal. As though that were even possible. His mastery of her in the bedroom was complete. Better to enjoy what he offered than to resist. She sank into the rhythm, meeting his hips in an upward thrust of her own, winding her tongue with his, and following the inexorable spiral up to the bliss he always brought her.

He rose to his knees, his long, insistent fingers clutching her sides, lifting her to his lap. Wrapped tightly in his arms, she rode him until, his voice hoarse, he said, "Come for me."

Once more she ground on his hard length, her gaze riveted to his face. His teeth were clenched as though he were in great pain. He was waiting for her. Gods, she loved him, this man who promised to always take care of her. Even here, where he demanded her complete submission, he put her needs first. Her orgasm hit, and rather than slump forward against him, she threw her head back, determined to watch when release claimed him.

Their gazes met. His eyes glowed with confidence and cocky satisfaction. One word fell from his lips. "Perfect."

Three times he thrust into her, pulling her tightly onto his pulsing erection. Darcelle melted under her own euphoria, reveling in the power she held over this man. Whether he knew it, she did. They were equals, each with different but balancing control over the other. Her fears had been baseless. Arguing over who was in charge in a relationship was pointless. They both were.

Matou fell sideways to the bed, drawing her with him still in his embrace. They lay, staring at one another. Darcelle was positive he would say something important. Instead he tapped a finger on her cheek.

"We have to get up. There's a job to plan and prepare for." He pulled her to a sitting position and slapped her thigh. "Go shower and dress in your room. Otherwise I won't keep my hands off you." He slid off the bed and headed to his en suite bathroom. "Now." Calm, cool, and collected Matou was back.

Darcelle found a shirt in Matou's closet and, with the hem floating around her at midthigh, dashed to her own room.

By the time she'd showered and changed into a casual dark blue shirt and denim pants, Matou was knocking. She opened the door to Mr. Three C's. That didn't bother her anymore. It was a facade. Underneath it was a passionate, sometimes playful man who could, at least with her, loosen his control.

"The others are waiting for us in the conference room downstairs."

Darcelle followed him, close to jogging to keep up with his long, rapid strides. The office complex was one level lower. Darcelle had been inside the tech safe room and Max's office, but the other workspaces, a few with palm locks, were a mystery to her. The tech safe room where Jeanne had trained Darcelle to use a variety of legal and illegal equipment was sealed against any imaginable intrusion and damage from electromagnetic strikes. Matou liked to be prepared for anything.

Inside the conference room, Cade, Max, Bassinae, and Jeanne were seated around a long table. Touch screens were embedded in front of each seat, and a large vidscreen covered the wall at the far end of the table. Darcelle took the empty chair next to Jeanne.

When Matou had seated himself at the near end, he took the time to look everyone in the eye before speaking. "Darcelle has completed her level two training in less time than I expected. That gives us an extra week to prepare."

Jeanne snapped at him. "You're sure she's ready?"

Matou turned his gaze on Jeanne. No hint of irritation showed. His tone was gentle when he responded. "I assure you, she's more than ready."

Jeanne was fiddling with the bracelet on her wrist. She stroked her hand up and down her arm before answering. "Okay. I...need to be sure."

"I understand. We're going to do this. Darcelle's help is indispensable. I couldn't have found a more perfect partner."

"It's just...you're sleeping with her." Jeanne eyed Darcelle.

"Another reason I wouldn't let her do this if she weren't ready."

"Okay." Jeanne released a deep breath. "Okay."

Matou moved his gaze to Darcelle. Intensity rolled off him. "The job I'm going to outline today is the reason I first pursued making you my partner. Your role is vital. I'm trusting you won't fail me. Failure is unacceptable. The stakes are much higher than regaining stolen art. We're going to take a child from a man who has no right to her, who stole her from her mother's custody."

Eyes blinking rapidly, Darcelle sat still for a moment to collect her fuzzy thoughts.

"Jeanne's daughter, Cheyenne. My niece. She's a sweet little girl who doesn't deserve to be away from her mother." He returned his attention to Jeanne. "I miss her, but I know you miss her more."

Darcelle looked at Jeanne, whose gaze was fixed on her index finger tracing the edge of her touch screen. *That explains a lot.* Her eyebrows knitted, Darcelle returned her attention to Matou and asked, "How soon?"

"In five weeks."

Caught up in the intensity that radiated from Matou, Darcelle shifted in her seat. That was soon. Was she ready? The last few weeks had been a game to her, demanding yet fun. Climbing, jumping, and avoiding detection were essential training to be a cat burglar. But she'd believed she'd be risking her own neck, not the future of a child. Could she do this? She resisted the urge to pull her hair tighter in its elastic, striving to maintain a placid face. "Explain."

Shoes scuffed under the table in the moment of silence that followed her request. "Twenty-one months ago, Jeanne's ex-lover, the father of her daughter, Cheyenne, kidnapped the girl, smuggling her off planet. He took her to Cantor 9 and received a grant of full custody from the planetary officials. Despite Jeanne's prior claim to full custody rights here, the Federation refuses to prioritize her claim without an extended legal battle that would take years. This has allowed the father, Antolle Westeen, to travel throughout the

Federation with Cheyenne without fear she would be taken from him by spaceport authorities."

A sigh threatened to expose her inner turmoil, but she eased it out. *To Jeanne she must seem nothing more than a dilettante, a cat burglar wannabe, more interested in getting into Matou's pants than anything else. But that's not true. I've trained hard, and if Matou says I'm ready, I am. He wouldn't risk something this important on an unprepared novice.*

Through eyes that had grown wintry, Matou glanced at each of them again.

"Westeen Resources, the family business, has its annual shareholders meeting in five weeks. Antolle has avoided it, but he has to be here for this one. It's the quadrennial full shareholders meeting which requires all stockholders to be present to vote. He and his family combined are majority stakeholders. He could still skip it, but if he does, his family's percentage of voting stock drops below the fifty percent mark, allowing nonfamily shareholders the opportunity to make changes the family has resisted. Changes that one new stockholder, Genetian Holding, has been pushing."

From the way the corner of his mouth lifted after his last statement, it was obvious the person behind the move to change the company's way of doing business was Matou himself. But if Cheyenne remained off planet, what did it matter if Westeen attended the meeting? Unless criminal charges had been pressed against him for kidnapping. But a trial here wouldn't force the government of Cantor 9 to return Cheyenne. The Federation didn't interfere with on-planet governance unless forced to by a Fed court.

"In addition to his own stock, Westeen claims the right to vote the stock left to Cheyenne by her great-grandmother, Benecia. Great-grandma didn't like Antolle, so she gave Jeanne the right to vote Cheyenne's shares by proxy. Westeen took Cheyenne so he could claim the right to vote his daughter's stock by dint of holding physical custody of Cheyenne."

"Until this year, Antolle's mother, Leona, Cheyenne's grandmother, has been voting all his and Cheyenne's stock by proxy. She's not pleased that he is subverting Benecia's dying wishes or with how he's using his own daughter as a business tool. Six months ago she informed Antolle that the largest nonfamily stockholder was insisting Jeanne be allowed to vote Cheyenne's stock unless he could verify that Cheyenne was in his custody, and Leona was supporting the request."

Eyes closed for a moment, Darcelle organized the information Matou had imparted. Great-grandma, grandma, father, daughter. Benecia, Leona, Antolle, Cheyenne. Antolle kidnapped his daughter so he could control the company shares left to Cheyenne by her great-grandmother. Sleazebag. He didn't really want Cheyenne. Darcelle could see why Grandma Leona was unhappy with her son.

Matou continued. "Westeen needs to vote Cheyenne's stock to put a stop to the nonfamily stockholder insurrection. He's not certain, as his mother seems to be, that Jeanne would vote with the family. Bringing Cheyenne here would put him in a tenuous position with the local authorities. He would have to come and go quickly and quietly. A director of Genetian Holding has agreed to visit Antolle's apartment to verify Cheyenne is in his custody before the meeting. That is planned for early the day of the annual meeting."

"So forcing him to bring Cheyenne down planet gives us the opportunity to kidnap her back." *Jeanne's lucky to have a brother as capable at intrigue as Matou is.* One more thing Darcelle found to admire about him.

"That's the idea. Once Jeanne has custody of Cheyenne, she will sell Cheyenne's stock to Genetian Holding. That paperwork has already been prepared. Jeanne might have done that before, but this avoids any ongoing legal battles."

"And that douchebag won't have reason to kidnap Cheyenne again," Jeanne snarled.

Around the table the others voiced their agreement.

"Westeen surrounds himself with tight security that includes nannies who are also trained bodyguards. As I noted, coming down planet with Cheyenne he has to make sure the local authorities don't discover she is with him."

Nothing about this sounds easy. Darcelle glanced at the others around the table. Each one looked competent, capable. Add two more *c's* to calm, cool, and collected. It wasn't just Matou. Each of these people had been judged proficient members of the team Matou had assembled. She was the last piece, the person requiring additional training. If she screwed up, she would be out. Despite having skipped breakfast, her stomach was heavy. If she didn't meet Matou's expectations, he would send her on her way. This thing that had started between them would die before it grew into something more. She would lose Matou.

Not happening. With a surreptitious shrug, she straightened her shoulders and focused on what Matou was saying.

"Westeen can accomplish that using a private shuttle to bring them from the spaceport to the residential tower owned by his family. The thirteenth floor holds his apartment. The other apartments in the building belong to other family members and high-level company staff. An underground shuttle hanger was added to the facility in the last year. Once she's through customs and onto his shuttle, it will be impossible to convince the *gendarmes* to take Cheyenne into their custody."

Darcelle bit her tongue to keep from interrupting with the obvious question. How could he get Cheyenne through customs without local officials finding out? She had to be on a missing children's list. Besides, the Feds required everyone traveling from their home planet into Fed space to have a passport.

"He'll be using a Cantor 9 passport for Cheyenne under the name Taylor Westeen. Without a court order, the police won't act."

Sneaky bastard.

"The time spent on planet will be as short as he can make it. I expect them to arrive down planet in the afternoon on the day before the meeting. There will be a banquet that evening which he will be expected to attend. Once the meeting concludes the next day, he will return to the spaceport as soon as possible. That leaves little time to pursue a court order to search his apartment while Cheyenne is there. We aren't ignoring that avenue of restoring Cheyenne to her mother, but it will likely fail. Our best option is to obtain entry to his apartment and take Cheyenne."

Darcelle stiffened her spine and met Jeanne's assessing gaze. She wanted a sign, added proof, that Darcelle was ready for this. Damn straight she was. Ready, willing, and able. She gave Jeanne a curt nod, which was returned.

Chin lifted a notch higher, she listened to Matou detail their mission.

"The plan I've come up with will require all of you. Let me begin by…"

CHAPTER NINE

DARCELLE STARED UP the side of the Westeen Residential Tower. It wasn't the tallest building in the city, but it overtopped the surrounding apartment piles. The night was dark, which was a break for them. A stiff breeze blew from the southwest, full of the scent of an impending storm. Matou stood several floors above and to her right on one of the jutting ledges that studded the building.

The original plan had been to reach Cheyenne's window by leaping from ledge to ledge, following a zigzagging path across the western face of the building. In preparation, some of the ledges had been recreated on the climbing wall in Matou's gym. After two weeks of practice, the distance between ledges had still been too great for Darcelle to clear.

A gust of wind slapped the belaying rope against her lower leg. She checked to assure the rope hadn't become tangled before returning her gaze to where Matou had set a belaying point and was preparing to leap. With the grace and power of a panther, he sprang for the next ledge, settling on the twelve-inch wide stone with ease. If he could have handled removing the child from her room and lowering her by himself, he wouldn't have needed Darcelle. But no ledges or handholds were available outside Cheyenne's window, so two people were needed to rescue her safely. Matou hadn't seemed frustrated with Darcelle's failure, but Jeanne had been another matter. Her former hostility toward Darcelle had returned in spades.

Darcelle's turn to climb came with three tugs on the belaying rope. The going was much slower, requiring her to set holds for hands and feet while she duplicated the route Matou had almost flown over. That effort helped calm the twitchiness of her nerves. The invisi-suits he had insisted they wear had apparently kept the occupants of the occasional vehicles that passed by from spotting her waiting at street level. This despite fullstrength headlights catching her in their beam. She'd seen it demonstrated, but like flying in hyperspace, what she didn't understand, she had to take on faith.

When she arrived at the anchor Matou had set, she sucked in air and scanned the side of the building up to where Cheyenne's window awaited. The small red point of a laser beam was positioned under the sill, pointing them to the correct spot. Matou had divided the climb into three pitches. They were one-third of the way up. With rapid efficiency they reset the belaying rope so he could continue climbing.

Darcelle leaned into the building. The wind was picking up, and gusts were more frequent and stronger. It was an effort to keep from clenching her abs, to relax muscles she'd be using soon. The nearly perfect landings Matou had made in the gym were impossible under these conditions, but he could still reach his designated perches well within the bounds of safety.

As Darcelle reached the second anchor point, splats of water dropped from the moisture-filled clouds burgeoning above them.

"We need to move faster. The rain won't hold off long," Matou shouted over the wind.

With a nod, Darcelle gave him a thumbs-up. Braced against the stiff breeze, she kept her gaze on Matou. He abandoned caution, leaping, setting a belay point, and leaping again, a nonstop stream of motion. An enormous gust of wind swept across the face of the building, and Darcelle's heart stopped. Matou had leaped before the gust struck and was now teetering on the edge of the last ledge from which they would hand climb to Cheyenne's window. The belaying rope would catch him if he fell, but what shape would he be in if he did? Time slowed for Darcelle while Matou bent forward, using his powerful core muscles to pull himself onto the ledge. He set the final anchor point and gave the rope three tugs.

Darcelle made the most of the positive effects of the adrenaline rush she'd experienced watching Matou come close to falling, employing the added strength and energy to power her way up. Matou pulled her up to the last ledge. Fat raindrops were spattering on them.

Matou clipped her into the anchor point and shouted, "Let's go." Minutes later they were nine feet higher. When they were secure, Matou tapped ready on his wrist unit. That was the signal for Jeanne to activate the replacement feed to the building's interior security monitors.

One minute later Bassinae and Cade assumed their roles as drunken visitors arriving early for an after bash at Boris Westeen's apartment. Boris was known for throwing wild parties, and his apartment was one level up. The pair had had a great deal of fun preparing for their role in the rescue. They even got a laugh out of Jeanne, but now, behind their slurred impersonations, they were deadly serious.

From the getaway car parked two blocks away, Jeanne replaced the security feed from Cheyenne's room with a loop of the little girl sleeping, while at the same time monitoring the actual feed. Cheyenne was alone in her room, tucked in bed. Jeanne flashed Matou the all clear.

While they'd waited for Jeanne's signal, Darcelle had pulled a paint bottle filled with solvent and a spray bottle of activator from pockets on her thighs. After handing the containers to Matou, she shifted to the side to give him room to work. He applied a thick coat of solvent to the plasti-glass of the window, handed her the paint bottle, and, while leaning as far away as circumstances allowed, sprayed activator over the solvent. The minute the mist hit, a chemical reaction dissolved the plasti-glass, causing it to melt over the frame of the window. Once the reaction was complete, Matou slapped a thin mat onto the sill, covering the still-solidifying goop.

The crew had practiced the timing of each stage of the operation. Once Jeanne informed Matou that Cheyenne's bedroom was clear, Matou and Darcelle needed five minutes to retrieve the little girl. Most of that was spent removing the window. Now they'd accomplished that, they couldn't turn back to wait for a better opportunity. Bassinae and Cade were three minutes into their act, which required them to make their way inside the front door and keep as many of the security staff as possible occupied with them.

Darcelle climbed over the sill, careful to keep her hands away from the edges of the mat. With a push and twist on the connectors, she disposed of the belaying rope they had used in their climb. Behind her Matou was prepping the lines they would use to rappel the side of the building. Before her a night-light in the far corner made the bed where Cheyenne slept visible. In seconds Darcelle was beside the little girl. Lashes feathered her cheeks, and dark, straight hair was mussed on her pillow. Darcelle pulled the tranq dispenser from her breast pocket.

The child chose that moment to wake up, gasping and crying out. "Who are you?"

"Shhh. I'm a friend of your mommy's here to take you home."

Cheyenne, chocolate-brown eyes wide, gripped the top of her blanket and responded with an almost inaudible whisper. "My mommy doesn't want me. Daddy said."

"Oh, sweetheart. She does want you. She's waiting downstairs in a car. Your uncle Sebastian is waiting at the window to take you down to her."

"Uncle Seb?"

"Yes. They've missed you so much. Will you come with me?"

"I miss my mommy."

"Your mommy will be so happy to see you. I'm going to have you breathe some sleepy medicine now. When you wake up, you'll be with your mommy. Okay?"

To reassure her, Darcelle placed her hand over the little girl's fingers and showed her the nasal dispenser. Except for a slight tremble, the girl didn't react when Darcelle placed it over her nose.

"Breathe deep."

In moments Cheyenne's head lolled to the side. Darcelle scooped her up and dashed to where Matou waited, his arms outstretched. The rain had finally become the threatened downpour, slicking Matou's hair against his skull. It shouldn't matter with the rope they were using, but the hand- and footholds Darcelle would use to climb out the window would be slick.

Once Cheyenne was firmly in Matou's grasp, Darcelle fastened safety webbing around the little girl to secure her to his chest, leaving his hands free. Darcelle watched him push off and descend. As soon as he was clear, she crouched on the sill and dropped one foot to search for a foothold.

Outside the bedroom a female voice shouted, "Get them out of here. I'm checking on Cheyenne."

Uh-oh. No more distraction.

The sound of the door opening reached Darcelle at the same moment her toe found the foothold. She planted her foot on it, glad it didn't slip. It was past time to be gone. Hands clamped tight to the sill, she drew her other leg up to swing outside. Something hard hit her calf, but she ignored it, crouching below the window. An arctic breeze blew along her spine at the sight of a woman pointing a gun at her. Without a second thought, Darcelle snatched the rope high over her head, pulled her knees up, and shoved her feet into the female bodyguard.

Relieved the woman had fallen backward, Darcelle threaded the rope around her feet and clamped one foot on top of the other. The bodyguard had scrambled up and was once again aiming at Darcelle. But she was already sliding out of sight, allowing herself to drop five stories before she braked. Above her a male voice spoke. "Don't shoot. You might hit Cheyenne. Comms are down. We have to get below and stop them."

Thank the gods. Getting shot was not on her to-do list. And then, twenty stories up, pain struck and with it, nausea. A searing agony speared from her lower leg to her groin. Had she been shot after all? Her head swimming, Darcelle struggled to stay conscious, forcing herself to move hand over hand, each movement excruciating. She had to hurry. Her vision was going black.

She awoke to the sensation of the rope sliding through her gloved hands, and reflexively gripped it tight. The inertia of her body's plunge to the street nearly pulled her arms from their sockets. The wind slapped the rope against her in the drenching rain. She no longer had a foothold. The pressure on her shoulders compelled her hands to open. She was going to die.

But she didn't drop. A powerful arm wrapped around her waist. "I've got you."

Matou! Thank the gods! "My leg…"

"I know. Relax. We're almost to the ground. Bassinae and Cade are pulling his car around. We need to hurry. Let me support you."

Darcelle slumped against him.

"That's it."

RIPPING THE WEBBING AWAY from Cheyenne while he ran for the waiting car, Sebastian repressed the victory cry that welled within him. They weren't there yet, but once Cheyenne was in the car, the chances for failure lowered significantly. The authorities wouldn't be called. That would ensnare Westeen in explanations he wanted to avoid. With the guards' comms unable to contact staff on the first floor, security was minutes behind them. Darcelle should be here any second.

The door of the car flung open to greet him. Sebastian kissed Cheyenne's forehead. A knot released inside his chest. He'd done it, brought his Cheyenne home to her mother. Jeanne swung out and wrapped Cheyenne in her arms when Sebastian passed her over. Tears were streaming down Jeanne's face when she looked up at Sebastian, but her huge smile transformed when her mouth dropped open and her eyes grew wide, her gaze fixed over his shoulder.

"Darcelle."

"What?" Sebastian turned. Darcelle was dangling high above, the rope knocking against her legs. She wasn't moving. She was in trouble.

Over his shoulder, Sebastian yelled at Max. "Get them to the penthouse. Tell Cade to pick us up." He sprinted to where the end of Darcelle's rope coiled on the pavement, leaped, grabbed the twisted cord over his head, and began to climb. When he leaned back to start his third move up the rope, he froze. Darcelle was sliding down. Why wasn't her descender stopping her? If she was having problems, all she had to do was release it and it would stop her automatically. But she wasn't stopping.

Nothing for it. He would have to break her fall. His heart pounding and his lungs pumping, superhuman strength flooded him. When she slammed into him, he would lose his grip. And although the distance to the ground from where he clung was only a story and a half, he would likely die from the double impact. But she might survive. He braced himself. The rope jerked violently, and an agonized scream sliced across his nerves.

But Darcelle's body didn't collide with him. She'd stopped herself—or the descender had—two feet above him. Whatever the cause of the miracle, he wouldn't lose the opportunity to get her the rest of the way to the pavement.

It was a moment and forever before he'd positioned himself to support her and had a hand around her midsection. Icy fingers wrapped his core. His legs went weak, and his energy drained like he'd been punched in the gut. Darcelle wasn't latched on to the descender. She'd been free climbing. If she hadn't... No, he wasn't going there. He needed to get her to the ground and find out what had gone wrong.

With deft fingers he strapped her against him with the webbing he'd used to secure Cheyenne to his torso. Darcelle was fading in and out. She no longer had a grip on the rope. She mumbled something about her leg. A vibration ran through the rope. Once. Twice. A third time. Cade was below, holding the line steady. Sebastian moved, hand over hand, resisting the pull of gravity and the need in his heart to slide and arrive below faster. What did the traffic sign say? Safety first. Speed next.

The sounds of voices and running feet came from the far corner of the building. If Cade hadn't been there, the invisi-suits he and Darcelle wore might have kept them hidden. Sebastian was a few feet above the ground, so he loosened his grip and dropped. Cade helped him balance when his feet hit the pavement. The two men and a woman who were racing toward them, guns drawn, were about one hundred feet away.

"That's not Cheyenne he's holding. It's the one I shot." The woman stopped and aimed her weapon. "Hands on your heads, or I shoot."

Her companions thundered on, blocking her from making good on her threat.

With Darcelle's back strapped to his chest, Sebastian wrapped his arms around her and carried her to the aircar. Bassinae stood with the door open, slamming it shut the moment after Sebastian had flung himself and Darcelle into the backseat. Bassinae jumped through and slammed her own door. Cade was already at the wheel. Once Bassinae was inside, he hit the locks. A thud shook the car. One man had slammed into the side of the car and was attempting to enter the vehicle. Cade took off vertically, speeding away. The mirror on the right side of the car shattered, but the gunshots caused no further damage to the reinforced chassis and windows of the vehicle.

Sebastian instinctively huddled over Darcelle, who lay unconscious in his arms. The crack of bullets sounded around them, stilling when Cade had driven out of range. Sebastian fought through the fog in his brain. What had happened? After unfastening the webbing, he ripped his gloves off and transferred Darcelle from his lap, placing her to lie along the seat. His hand came back bloody. What the fuck! She was soaking wet and shivering. On his knees beside her, he ran his hands over her, searching for more wounds. Bassinae offered a blanket to him. He spread it over Darcelle, tucking it around her but leaving her right leg, where she was bleeding, exposed.

"Raise her feet." Bassinae's voice sounded urgent. "Raise her feet. She's in shock."

"She's been shot in the leg. The backside of her leg's been blown away. She's losing blood."

Rustling and clattering sounded from the front seat. Bassinae shoved the medikit case over Sebastian's shoulder. "Check for a broken bone. If nothings broken, prop her feet on this. I'll hand you a pair of scissors. Cut away her pant leg."

Sebastian followed her directions. *At least someone is thinking clearly. Even if I'm not.* A cloth was nudged against his hand.

"Dry her leg as best you can with this. Then wrap this dressing around her leg, covering as much of the wound as possible."

Bassinae held out a hemostatic pressure bandage. Darcelle hadn't reacted while Sebastian worked on her, but when he applied the bandage, she cried out and tugged her leg away from him.

"Sorry, minou. I need to stop the bleeding. You've been shot."

She mumbled something unintelligible. He finished as swiftly as possible. Pain pierced his heart each time she shrieked and flinched from his touch.

"It's going to be okay. I'm going to take care of you." He flung his next words over his shoulder to Cade. "Get us to the hospital."

"Almost there, sir."

"I've called ahead. They'll meet us at the emergency doors." Bassinae's voice was soothing, but nothing except seeing Darcelle smiling and healthy could assuage the ache in his chest. He'd stopped most of the bleeding, but the blood seeped from around the edges. The urge to give way and bellow in anguish pushed at him. He'd be damned if he lost his self-control now when he needed it most. Holding Darcelle's hand, he rattled soothing phrases. She was so cold, her skin clammy. When he took her pulse, it was weak.

"How much longer?" He bellowed the question, but Darcelle didn't stir.

"One more block, sir. A right turn and then I'll be pulling up in front of emergency."

The hospital staff poured out of the building while Cade brought the car to a stop. They swiftly took over. Darcelle was on a gurney and inside before Sebastian could do more than stammer, "She's been shot. Please help her."

A woman shunted him to an admin desk when he tried to follow the med techs taking Darcelle through a set of password-coded doors. For the first time since he'd been a child, tears streamed down his face. He'd nearly lost her. Gods. What if she'd died? She could still die. Slumped forward, he threaded his fingers through his hair and pulled the damp strands back. He had to get control of himself.

"Sir. She's in the best hands. Try not to worry."

He released his head and straightened. "Not easy."

"No." Her sympathetic tone changed to a brisker one. "Why don't we get the paperwork out of the way? It might distract you until the doctor tells us what's happening."

"All right." It wasn't possible to restrain his mind from rehashing tonight's events or from worrying about Darcelle.

CHAPTER TEN

DARCELLE WAS IN surgery for over an hour. Sebastian, Cade, and Bassinae waited in the standby room, silence stifling them. Max showed up right before the doctor delivered his postoperative chat.

"Mr. St. Croix. Ms. Lebeau suffered a soft-tissue impact through the calf muscle of her right leg. The posterior tibial artery was not damaged. There was no bone involvement. After debridement of the wound, it was treated for infectious agents. Much of her calf muscle was destroyed. I sealed the exposed areas with steri-skin. Ms. Lebeau was given the first of a series of four nanite infusions to speed regrowth of the muscle tissue and healing of the wound. Physical therapy will be required for both the leg and for her shoulders due to tendon damage. Expected full recovery in two to four weeks. She is under sedation for twelve hours to allow the steri-skin to integrate. It can be a painful treatment, so we usually sedate patients during the process."

Cade, Bassinae, and Max returned home once Darcelle was taken to a room on the surgical recovery floor. Seated beside her bed in a chair designed to conform to the body of its occupant, clasping her hand, Sebastian fought drowsiness. Adrenaline, stress, and fear combined to create a fatigue that made his body ache. Sometime during the twelve hour wait for Darcelle to come out of sedation, he fell asleep.

"Sebastian."

Someone whispered his name again.

"Sebastian."

He roused, opening his eyes, confused for a moment. "Sebastian."

Misty gray eyes were staring at him. "You're awake." The tears he'd thought he had under control returned.

"Mmm."

The normally rosy-brown luster of her skin was washed out by an unhealthy pallor. She had never been more beautiful.

"Where am I?"

Matou wiped his face. "You're in hospital."

Her gaze roamed the room.

He grasped her hand. "You were shot."

"Shot?"

"You don't remember?"

A wrinkle formed between her eyebrows. "I remember pain. And my head being all woozy." Her eyes widened. "I...I fell."

Chest tightening at the memory, he choked out, "You caught yourself."

"And you were there."

He swallowed hard. "I was." His hand trembled when he reached out and brushed her cheek with his knuckles. "I'll always be there."

Her expression softened. "That's good."

The anger he'd felt when learning she hadn't used her safety descender slipped out. "Someone needs to be, if you insist on ignoring safety measures."

"I didn't have time. She had a gun."

Sebastian's chest tightened with pain. "That's one of your nine lives gone. I'm going to make sure you don't lose any more."

Her lips lifted in a hint of a smile. "You do like to be in charge. I don't mind. It shows you love me."

"I do. I love you, Darcelle. More than I ever believed possible."

He didn't need her to tell him he loved her. It was blatantly obvious even to an avowed bachelor like him. But it created a struggle within him. Pack her in cotton batting and control everything she did, so she'd always be there for him—or recognize he couldn't regulate everything in her life and instead devote himself to making sure she had everything necessary to keep her safe? If he dominated every aspect of her life, she would no longer be the woman he loved. Strong. Capable. Sassy. And blazing hot in a tub full of bubbles. He needed that woman. He loved her.

A flush of pleasure brightened her pale cheeks. "You called me Darcelle."

"That's your name?"

"You've always called me minou. I like that, too, but it's… You see me. The real me. Not who you think I should be or who you want me to be. But me."

Sebastian stood, bent over the bed, and brushed a kiss over her lips. With his gaze fixed on hers, he said, "I do see you. Every wonderful bit of you. I no longer want to make you my partner."

Darcelle's eyebrows rose.

"I need *you* to make *me* your partner. I can't get along without you, minou."

"As your partner in crime?"

Sebastian winced. "Maybe. Probably. We both have a taste for cat burglary. But no, not just in crime, in everything. Every tomcat needs a minou of his own."

"And kittens." Darcelle's laughter tinkled. "You should see your face."

"I'd never thought about…children. I'm not sure—" He was baffled by the tendril of pleasure that wrapped around his heart.

"Are we in trouble?"

"No. At least not much." He tried to keep his expression light. "I took care of it."

"Mmm. Did Jeanne and Cheyenne get away?"

"Yes. Max got them to the penthouse. Safe and secure."

She looked at the window, but it was covered. "Is it morning yet?"

After a quick check of the time, he said, "It is. They kept you asleep for twelve hours after surgery. You slept longer than that. It's going on noon."

"But we won. Jeanne and Cheyenne will be together. Right?"

"Yeah. Jeanne signed the paperwork to sell Cheyenne's shares in

Westeen Resources. Max said the announcement that Genetian Holding owned that voting stock created a significant stir at the annual meeting."

Darcelle flashed a hint of a smirk. "Significant, huh?"

His own smile cocky, Sebastian grunted. "That's what Max said. The shareholders voted to remove Antolle from the board, replacing him with a member of Genetian Holding's board. Westeen stormed out, but Leona Westeen seems to be taking it in stride. She asked the woman from Genetian to take Antolle's seat beside her. They had their heads together while additional business was conducted, and left together for the luncheon."

"Are the authorities going to pursue kidnapping charges against Antolle?"

"That's yet to be determined. But I at least intend to take steps to sever his parental rights in Federation court. He's given us plenty of ammunition. Westeen Resources shareholder meetings are recorded, and he had plenty to say when he found out he'd lost all chance of controlling Cheyenne's stock."

"Good."

He cocked his head to the side. "But you haven't asked me to be your partner yet. Are you going to make me wait? Make me jump through hoops?"

A gradual smile lit her face. "There is precedence for hoop jumping. Maybe a little training." Her eyes lit with a brilliant ferocity. "Will you be my partner, Sebastian St. Croix?"

His whole body went still. Even his heart paused for a moment as joy filtered through his entire being. "As long as forever lasts, I'm yours." He bent and kissed her, restraining the physical outpouring of his passion for this woman, his minou, his Darcelle. He had plenty of time to make love to her. She was his future.

"Come snuggle with me."

"I don't want to hurt you."

She smiled faintly. "You won't hurt me. The bed has plenty of room, and I'm doped to my eyeballs on pain meds."

"Well then." Sebastian took off his boots and climbed in beside her, lying on his side, and, after pulling a fluff of curls away, resting his head against hers.

"I love you, Sebastian, my Matou."

"I love you, Darcelle, my minou."

Sebastian smiled. Even in a hospital bed, life couldn't be better.

THE END

Thanks for reading! Please add a review on Amazon and let me know what you thought!

Also by Cailin Briste

Sons of Tallav Series

Shane: Marshal of Tallav

Shane Tiernan, the Beast of Tallavan aristocratic society, needs relief from the matriarchal rules that are destroying his life. His hope lies in a female submissive, newly graduated from a top sex school. From her resume, she seems perfect. Profile and real life collide when he arrives to collect her. He's stunned when he spots her vaulting over a bar and snatching up an ice chipper to defend herself against the giant who is chasing her. Her combination of warrior spirit and long-limbed curves fires his Dom imagination and the desire to bind her in his rope and have her under his complete control.

Adrianna Pacquin is sexually submissive, but don't cross her outside the bedroom. She's escaped the crime lord who plans to marry her once before. When it becomes clear he's still after her, she doesn't intend to get caught. A fortuitous decision to accept the contract of Tallavan Marshal Shane Tiernan promises safety until an attempt to murder him sets the pair on an investigation that will require complete trust in one another. With danger stalking their every step, the secrets they both hide could implode their blooming relationship and leave them exposed to their relentless foe.

Maon: Marshal of Tallav

Maon Keefe has always been told he's doomed to fail as a husband. He decides never to marry instead focusing on living life as a player and becoming a capable marshal of Tallav. When he is shot and the most-wanted criminal he's escorting escapes, he fears that his career, his one success in life, is doomed. Assigned to ferret out the cause of missing shipments for a VIP aristocrat, he meets Selina Shirley CEO of the House of Shirley. He finds himself inexplicably attracted to her despite her frumpy appearance. When he meets a hooded and masked, scorching hot Domme, Lasair, at his friend's BDSM club, he's torn between the two women. Both fire his imagination and call to his submissive nature. Either might be the woman to change him into successful husband material.

Selina Shirley organizes her life like she organizes her business, taking control of all aspects of each. She's concluded that she must marry to get an heir and that her future husband must be totally submissive. Mentored by the sector's most famous sadist, she learns what it takes to be a proper Domme. Then, hidden behind a hood and mask, as Lasair, she meets Maon and her instant attraction to his full submission at the BDSM club leads her to break her own rules and become involved with him. But he's also the marshal assigned to investigate thefts at her company. When his broad streak of protective alpha male comes into play, it obvious he's not a 24/7 submissive. To stick to her plan to marry the perfect husband, she must ignore her heart and dump Maon.

Rand: Son of Tallav
Available July 17, 2018

Randolph Meryon is a man no woman can resist despite the whip and title of sadist he brandishes. A pariah on his home planet of Tallav, he created a new life on Beta Tau, opening a kink club, The Whip Hand. The club is wildly successful, making him the most well-known and richest sadist in the sector. Old scandal comes roaring back into his life when his sister dies, and he's compelled to return to Tallav where his mother expects him to become guardian to his niece.

Jen O'Malley, reeling from the consequences of her own, more recent disgrace, must find employment. But shunned by the O'Malley family, her attempt to find work without their backing meets barriers on all sides. A position as nanny with the scandal-riddled Meryon family seems like a lifeline. She's relieved until she arrives at Briarcliff and falls under the spell of Randolph Meryon.

Next in the A Thief in Love Suspense Romance Series

How to Steal the Pharaoh's Jewels

Release Date: April 23, 2018

Cade's fantasy is to seduce his best friend if he isn't murdered first.

His comfortable routine as a member of Sebastian St. Croix's cat burglar team is shattered the day he's pinned in a crushed car. In a moment of clarity, before everything goes dark, he realizes he's in love with his best friend, a woman who has sworn off intimate relationships for life.

It's taken Bassinae years to overcome a past filled with physical abuse and embrace the truth that she is a powerful, capable woman in her own right. Tamping down a case of nerves, she's ready to take on a larger role as a thief in Sebastian's next caper. If only Cade would stop acting like a lovelorn idiot. She needs her best friend's support to help steal the Pharaoh's jewels.

Set in the distant future, this sci-fi suspense romance has action and adventure as well as a sizzling romance.

A short excerpt from How to Steal the Pharaoh's Jewels

The main throughway to the spaceport was snarled in gridlock, so Cade diverted the car to a slower but better regulated side street. He made this trip frequently enough that he had the route and its alternates memorized down to the timing of the automated signals.

Still he would have preferred the quicker course of an open throughway.

His conversation with Bassinae yesterday replayed in his mind. Was she really so dissatisfied with her life that she'd quit her job at Do It Now? What would that mean for her role as a member of Sebastian's burglary team? Hell, what would it mean to no longer have his best friend and the most important woman in his life no longer right next door. Fate couldn't be that cruel. And now, this road was jammed two intersections ahead.

"Damn traffic!" He slapped his palm on the padded steering wheel. In the old days no one got in his way. But then he'd been wearing battle armor as a peacekeeper for the United Colonies. Nothing like fear to clear citizens from your path.

"Problem?" The deep voice resonating from the back seat was Sebastian St. Croix, Cade's boss and the man who had taken Cade in when the military had cast him on the trash heap.

"No. Intersection's blocked ahead. I'll go another street right. We'll get there in plenty of time."

"Do what you have to. You know how my mother hates to stand around and wait. If we're not there, she'll take a cab, and I'll hear about it for the next two weeks."

Cade chuckled. "I'll try to keep you out of trouble." Sebastian's mother was a force of nature. Nothing stopped her from doing as she pleased except for her husband, Sebastian's father. The man was the immovable object that when necessary blocked her irresistible drive forward. The only time Cade had been a witness to such a set down his admiration for the man's authority had grown immensely. But Gerald St. Croix was the only person alive who had that effect on his wife.

The woman refused to use shuttle flights on planet even though she was wealthy enough to afford them. One should never take to the air when traveling short distances. This was her dictum based in theory on energy savings. Not that there was any substantial difference in fuel cost between ground and shuttle traffic. She'd grown up on a colony planet that had suffered near catastrophic power loss from the shoddy infrastructure installed by political crooks. To this day she insisted on saving energy when it didn't overly hinder her pampered lifestyle. Thus, collecting her from the spaceport took an hour long drive rather than a fifteen-minute flight.

With a grunt of approval, Cade noted the route change had worked. The road ahead was less congested, so he relaxed back into his seat and picked up speed. A parking garage lined the left side of the street with office buildings on the right. He checked the time and glanced in the rear-view mirror. "Want some music?"

At that moment a large dump truck came barreling out of an exit of the parking garage. Cade swung right and hit the brakes hard, hoping to lessen the inevitable impact. Safety foam inundated the foot wells of the car, and the air ballasts deployed. The scree of metal and the splintering of the car's plastic shell, filled Cade's ears along with a sound like the roaring thunder of thousands of wild animals stampeding toward him. One thought struck him. *No pain.* And then the world winked out.

ABOUT THE AUTHOR

Cailin Briste writes science fiction suspense romance. Her first series is set in the Tallavan sector of the Federation where the men of Tallav are the marshals that provide protection and justice to the planets in this far off the beaten path area of space. While fighting crime, they also must come to terms with the matriarchal system of their home planet, Tallav. Tricky because each is heavily involved in the BDSM lifestyle. Book one is her Dom, book two is her male submissive, and book three due out in July 2018 is her sadist.

Her second series, A Thief in Love Suspense Romance series, begins with a cat burglar who puts together a team to steal priceless art and antiquities from other thieves. Sebastian is a Robin Hood character whose Maid Marion is his equal on the rooftops of their futuristic city. The second in the series is the love story of two others on his team, Cade and Bassinae. Once again the team are breaking into someone's home to take back something that rightfully belongs to someone else, but this time they are also trying to stop a murder.

More books in each series are coming as is a new series about a pair of dragon shifters hatched from the same egg and the man they love, bounty hunter Brody Simmons.

More about Cailin's books can be found on her website at http://cailinbriste.com.

Or join her newsletter at http://cailinbriste.com/cailins-newsletter-sign-up/.

Follow Cailin on:
Facebook: www.facebook.com/cailinbriste/
Pinterest: www.pinterest.com/cailinbriste/

Goodreads:
www.goodreads.com/author/show/7413817.Cailin_Briste
Bookbub: www.bookbub.com/authors/cailin-briste
0GSX9QVW